The Saddle Club

The Saddle Club

Anya Nicole

Urban Books, LLC
78 East Industry Court
Deer Park, NY 11729

ISBN 13: 978-1-61793-546-6

Printed in the United States of America

The Saddle Club

by

Anya Nicole

This book is dedicated to my daughter, Sydney.
You are the light of my life. Everything I do, I do for you.

Acknowledgments

First and foremost, I would like to thank God for giving me the talent to write and providing me with the opportunity to share my stories with others.

I want to thank Urban Books for continuing to give me the opportunity to publish my work.

To my family: I love you all. You have helped shape me into the person I have become and, as I get older, I realize that nothing is more important than my family.

To my mother: There's not a day that goes by that I don't think about you or wish that you were still here with me. I love you!

To Shalena: You are the only person I can share my deepest thoughts with! You understand me and you never scold me for being who I am. I love you, babe!

To Sharmina: Thank you for being my superwoman! Words cannot describe how much I appreciate you in my life.

To Iris: You are the best! Thanks for always being there for me and supporting my dreams! Thanks for reading everything I send you!

To Margaret: Best friends forever . . . enough said! Love ya!

To Wavey: Thank you for your insight and support! Thank you for reading my manuscripts before I turn them in!

To Lenard: Thank you for coming back into my life; having you around means the world to me. You brought

Acknowledgments

me back home and made me realize that you never should forget where you came from. Love ya! Smooches!

To my readers: Thank you for your support and honest feedback! I love writing and I will continue to try my hardest to deliver entertaining stories while continuing to hone my craft.

Prologue

Keon rubbed his chapped hands together and shoved them back in his jacket pockets. He scanned the park and noticed that even the animals that resided there seemed to be absent. The only noise that could be heard, for what seemed like miles, came from one lonely owl perched above the leafless tree where he and Rafiq had chosen to dump their package. The owl's large, translucent golden eyes peered through Keon's guilty soul and when it hooted, chills ran down Keon's spine.

He grabbed the shovel from the back of the U-Haul pickup truck he and Rafiq rented a few hours before. With only the faint glow from the truck's lights to guide him, Keon sighed as he thrust the shovel into the frozen December ground and lifted out the first bit of dirt. He knew this was a bad idea but, after all, he did break the rules. For as long as he had worked for Lavender, he'd never messed up like this. Falling for a client was out of the question but he just couldn't help himself; the sex they had went from being a cold fuck to warm, intimate lovemaking.

"Chill out, man," Rafiq said, leaning against the back of the U-Haul. "It'll be over before you know it and we can all go back to living our lives."

Rafiq studied the sweat beading on Keon's brow; he was definitely shaken. It didn't take much to talk Keon into doing a dirty deed. All he needed to do was remind him that he would end up back in the pen where he had already spent three years. No nigga wanted to go back after doing that kind of time, or *any* time to be exact.

Rafiq dug into the back pocket of his dark denim True Religion jeans and pulled out a blunt and a cigarette lighter. He ran his lips across the edge of the cigar paper as if he were sealing an envelope to make sure it was nice and tight. Rafiq then lit it up, allowing the smoke to fill the cool winter air. He took a few short drags and exhaled without the slightest sign of choking. He continued to toke on the blunt, watching as Keon shoveled away, not thinking once to step in and help him. Rafiq had taken care of the hard part—burying the body was the grunt work.

"Take a hit of this." Rafiq held the lit blunt out to Keon. "It'll calm you down."

Keon stared at the burning blunt, noting the weird smell emanating from it. He hesitated for a moment and then took the blunt from Rafiq's gloved hand. He held it in between his index finger and his thumb and laid his lips upon it as if he were kissing a virgin girl for the first time.

"What's in this shit?" he asked, instantly feeling lightheaded. His eyesight blurred and a harsh burning sensation built up in his throat. He squatted down to the ground in hopes of trying to gain back his senses, but lost his balance and landed on his ass. He coughed violently and beat on his chest, hoping to clear his lungs.

"Angel dust," Rafiq replied coldly. "Now either take another hit or pass me my shit back."

Keon held the blunt out to Rafiq, who grabbed it from his hand.

Rafiq immediately took another toke from the blunt and laughed. "Stop bitchin'. A little dust ain't never hurt nobody."

Rafiq closed his eyes as he inhaled. He'd smoked so much of it that, to him, it was like smoking a regular bag of weed. He held the blunt out to Keon, who was struggling to get up from the ground.

Without thinking twice, Keon seized the blunt and finished it off with three long drags. He threw the stump to the ground and took a deep breath, allowing the high to consume his body. If he was going to get through the night, he needed to be on. He snatched the shovel from the ground and continued digging, but this time choosing to pick up the pace.

Rafiq folded his arms and watched as Keon dug a hole like a man possessed. *That's it. Just keep doing what you doing,* Rafiq thought with a sly grin spread across lips.

After two long hours of digging, Keon finally finished, stopping briefly here and there to warm his hands. He tossed the shovel up from the hole and climbed out. It wasn't as deep as he would have liked it to be, but the bitter winter air was starting to get the best of him. Plus, he wanted to get home before anybody realized he was gone.

Keon half walked, half jogged over to the U-Haul, pulled open the back of the pickup truck, and began tugging at the rolled-up carpet, which had to weigh over 140 pounds. He lugged it off the truck and stopped to catch his breath.

"Can I get a little help?" Keon asked, dragging it toward the hole.

Rafiq clasped his hands together, making sure his gloves fit correctly, before grabbing one side of the carpet. Together, they hoisted it off the ground and rushed over to the freshly dug hole to drop it in. The carpet plunged to the bottom, landing with a loud thump.

Rafiq ran to the passenger side of the truck, then returned to Keon's side with a long metal flashlight that he pointed down the hole. The beam of light exposed that the duct tape, which had been wrapped around the carpet, had broken loose, revealing Toni's lifeless, bruised body. Her battered face was stained with red streaks, and two swollen eyes revealed the agony of her ordeal. Burgundy-colored dried blood lay caked around her once graceful neck and surrounded what had been a crisp white pillowcase used to take her last breaths.

Keon couldn't hold it in any longer. He stepped away from the hole and vomited what was left of the turkey and cheese hoagie he'd eaten for lunch. He wiped his mouth with the sleeve of his leather jacket, leaving fragments of his stomach contents on the cuff.

"Don't worry, my man, we did a good thing," Rafiq said, patting him on the shoulder in reassurance. "We would all be in jail if she would have given us up."

Rafiq switched the flashlight to his other hand, and held it steadily over the hole as Keon picked up his shovel.

As Keon collected himself and threw the first bit of dirt into the hole, he stared in shock as the dark bits and pieces of the earth covered Toni's distorted face. A tear swept down his left cheek as he prayed for God's forgiveness.

Chapter 1

Paroled
December, 2007
Keon

Keon stood in the courtyard of Graterford Prison and waited patiently for the corrections officer to unbolt the gates. He looked up at the fortress-like cement walls that surrounded him and let out a loud sigh of relief. He'd already spent three long years and a day behind bars; he didn't mind waiting a few more minutes to get out. The corrections officers, armed with pistols at their hips, ushered him toward the exit. As the final gates parted, Keon cleared his parched throat and jostled his sweaty hands inside the pockets of his light blue denim Rocawear jeans, which were the style in 2004.

"You're free to go," the officer said, impatiently waiting for Keon to step outside the gates so he could get back to his mid-morning coffee break.

"Yeah . . . you right. I am free to go," Keon said, almost hesitantly.

He looked at the guard as if needing official approval that he was, indeed, a free man. The guard nodded, giving Keon the affirmation he sought in order to leave the premises. As he took his first few steps as a free man, Keon inhaled the fresh morning air. He closed his eyes and allowed the sun to beam down on his scruffy-bearded face. *Today is a new day,* Keon thought. He no longer had to abide by the rules of the system. Well, at least that's how it would be once he finished his parole. Keon stared down the dirt road leading up to the prison. There wasn't a car within a mile of his view. He was confident that his boy, Marquise, would be there to meet him as he promised earlier in the week. He looked down at the fake Rolex he just placed on his arm several minutes before; it read one P.M. It was then that he realized that the battery had stopped working from years of disuse. *Leave it to Marquise to be late,* Keon thought. He kicked at the tar-colored bits of gravel, trying to decide what he wanted more—a cheesesteak from Jim's or some pussy. If he could have both at the same time it would be a dream come true.

Keon's thoughts were quickly interrupted by Jay-Z's "Roc Boys (And the Winner Is) . . ." blaring from Marquise's silver smoked-out BMW 760Li with chrome wheels. The car rolled up beside him and he rolled the window down just enough for Keon to see his lopsided, sly grin.

"What's up, nigga?" Marquise yelled, positioning the car in park. He jumped out and walked around to give his homie a hug followed by a strong handshake.

"Man, I was starting to think you wasn't going to show," Keon said, shoving his hands back in his jeans pockets.

"Go 'head with that shit. You know we been cool way too long for me to do you greasy like that," Marquise said, leaning against the car and folding his arms across his chest. Marquise looked Keon over and then said, "Damn, nigga, I see you got your weight up."

When he got down to his boy's sneakers, he noticed Keon was wearing a pair of leaned-over Air Forces that used to be white but now were a light shade of gray. "I almost forgot," Marquise said, walking around the side of the car and opening the door. He reached into the back seat and pulled out a green and tan shoebox. He returned to his friend. "Here, man," he said, holding out the box to Keon. "You ain't going nowhere with me in them dogged-assed sneakers."

Keon took the box from his hand. "Thanks, man." He peered inside. His eyes fixed on a fresh pair of Timberlands in a size eleven. Keon grinned as he tucked the box under his arm and strolled toward the front passenger side of the BMW and opened the door.

"Wait a minute, homie," Marquise said, forcefully shutting the door, almost jamming Keon's fingers in the process. "I *told* you, you can't wear them bullshit-assed sneakers if you going to hang with me. Take them muthafuckas off right now and put them boots on."

"You serious?" Keon asked, easing around Marquise, again reaching for the car door handle.

"Hell yeah, nigga—dead serious," Marquise said, pushing Keon away and leaning against the door so he couldn't get in the car.

"And what am I supposed to do with these?" Keon asked, looking down at his sneakers, realizing that they were, indeed, dogged.

"Leave them shits right here on the side of the road," Marquise said, walking around to the driver's side.

Keon shook his head and slid his feet out of the sneakers, revealing a huge hole in one of the heels of his dingy off-white socks. Keon stepped into the boots and laced them up. The fit was perfect. Marquise had sent him a couple of pairs of sneakers while he was locked down so he knew his size.

"Now, can I get in the car?" Keon asked, grabbing the door handle.

"Yeah, nigga, you can get in now." Marquise chuckled. "But, for real, I shouldn't let you get in my car with them old-ass Rocawear jeans you wearin'. And I ain't even gonna get on your sorry-ass white T. I'ma save that for another day."

Keon sucked his teeth. "Fuck you, man. This the first time I put on real clothes in three years." He opened the door and slid in beside Marquise.

Marquise shook his head, laughing. "Nigga, them ain't real clothes you got on. I don't even know what to call that shit."

The lavish tan leather seats swallowed Keon whole. The fresh new-car smell filled his nose, as did the tantalizing aroma of high-grade weed. Keon shook his head. "After all these years you still ain't learn your lesson about smoking that shit."

Marquise shrugged, still grinning. "What can I say? Old habits die hard. Ya mean?" He eased his foot off the break and pulled off without checking his mirrors.

"Nigga, ya old habit is what got me locked up in the first place," Keon said, staring at the prison in the side-view mirror as it became smaller and smaller before disappearing from his view. Keon laid his head on the lush headrest and closed his eyes. *If I ever see that prison again, it will be too soon,* he thought. At that moment, Keon promised himself that no one or nothing could ever make him go back inside those walls.

"Damn, man, how many times you want a nigga to apologize for that shit? I told you I would take care of you once you got out and here I am. So stop trippin' on me," Marquise said, glancing at Keon, then refocusing his attention on the road.

"I know, man. I just thought you would have given *that* shit up by now. I mean, you in the fuckin' NBA, you got everything you could ever want, money, clothes, bitches, everything," Keon said, staring at the burned-up blunt in the ashtray.

Marquise's eyes followed Keon's gaze. He breathed heavily. "Well, being in the NBA ain't like what you think it is. I gotta work so much harder than these other niggas 'cause of my knee injury. I got so much fuckin' pressure on my ass right now just to keep my startin' position."

"Yo, remember that night?" Keon asked, looking over in Marquise's direction.

"What night?" Marquise asked, knowing exactly what he was talking about. He knew it was only a matter of time before Keon brought it up.

"The night I got locked up, nigga, what else would I be talking about?"

"Come on, man, that was over three years ago. I can't remember everything," Marquise said nonchalantly.

"Well I remember, that night changed my life. We was celebrating my birthday."

"Yeah, I remember we had just left the club and was heading to the after hour at the Motorcycle Club in South West," Marquise said blandly. Marquise remembered everything about that night. He just didn't want to talk about it. He knew that at some point it was going to come up, but he figured the less he acted as if he remembered, the better.

"Yeah, and we got pulled over by them two female cops. I knew as soon as that fat, little light-skinned bitch got out the car there was going to be trouble," Keon said, folding his hands in front of him on his lap.

"Yeah, she did seem to have it in for us and shit. The tall brown-skinned jawn was on me hard like she was ready to give me some pussy; she was going to let us go. But that other one, she was looking to send a nigga up," Marquise said, reaching up to adjust his rearview mirror.

"I'll never forget that bitch . . . Officer Ortiz. You know that little fat-ass ho had the prettiest green eyes I ever seen. I ain't never seen no Rican wit' no green eyes. I couldn't help but to stare at her when she shined that fuckin' flashlight in my face," Keon said, reliving the event in his mind.

"Damn, nigga, you really remember all dat shit? I was way too high that night to remember what the bitch looked like," Marquise said, shaking his head. "All I remember is the bitch being fatter than a mutha-fucka."

"I bet you remember her hitting you in the back of your knees with that fuckin' baton. You was cryin' like a little bitch," Keon said jokingly.

"Get the fuck outta here," Marquise said, flagging him and returning his hand to the wheel. Marquise twitched, thinking about how bad the baton had stung that night.

"You know I told you to get rid of that gun a long time ago," Keon said, getting serious for a moment. He looked straight ahead at the road.

"Do we gotta talk about this? That shit in the past," Marquise mumbled.

"For you it's in the past. I'm the one took the rap for your little store robbery and shootout," Keon hissed like a venomous snake. "Who the hell robs a fucking deli anyway? You knew them Chinks was gonna be armed."

"Damn, man, so you just going to throw me under the bus like that? I made a mistake; I needed a couple of dollars in my pocket and I ain't know where else to get it from."

"A mistake?" Keon asked, raising his voice. "That mistake got me locked down. I did that time for you be-cause I knew there was no way you was going to make it in jail. You my nigga and all but you too much of a loose cannon; you'da left the pen in a body bag."

"So what you trying to say, I'm a nut?" Marquise asked, raising his voice.

"I ain't say all that, I'm saying you ain't built for jail." Realizing that Marquise was getting upset about the conversation, Keon decided to just let it go. "So when you get this wheel?" Keon asked, easing off the subject.

"Nigga, this ain't my wheel. I graduated to Bentleys two years ago. This car is for you, playboy. It's the least I can do."

"For me?" Keon repeated, making sure he had heard him right.

"Yeah, nigga, you. I copped it a month ago after your parole hearing. As soon as I heard you was being released, I had to get you a welcome home present."

Keon ran his hand across the genuine wood finish; it was as smooth as a baby's ass. He leaned his head against the headrest and closed his eyes. "I can't keep this car, man. If my parole officer gets wind of this I'll be right back where I started off."

"I'll tell you what," Marquise said, merging onto the highway. "I'll keep it for you. And when you get offa parole, it's yours. Is that cool?"

"Hell yeah, that's cool," Keon agreed.

Marquise turned the satellite radio to Shade 45, and 50 Cent's "Hustler's Ambition" quaked from the sound system. He bobbed his head to the music, swerving in and out of traffic on the highway with one hand on the wheel and the other on the gear shift.

"Where we going?" Keon asked, rolling the window down halfway to escape the weed smell.

"To my crib. Why? You got somewhere to be?" Marquise asked, letting out a soft chuckle.

"Naw, man. I'm just hungry as shit."

"Damn, you fucked me up for a minute with them dicked sneakers you had on. I almost forgot I had you a steak on the back seat."

"Would you get off that sneaker shit? I'm tired of hearing about it," Keon said, reaching in the back seat.

"It's probably cold by now but it shouldn't matter, you used to eating cold-ass food anyway."

"Man, fuck you. Just because I was in the pen don't mean I was eating cold-ass food," Keon sneered, ripping the foil off the steak and unmasking its mouthwatering aroma of fried onions, ketchup, and Cheez Whiz. His stomach grumbled as he took his first bite. He chewed slowly, savoring each and every flavor. His taste buds tingled as he swallowed his first bite. Ketchup and Hellman's Real Mayonnaise dripped down his hands as he went in for a second bite.

Marquise glanced over at Keon. "The way you acting over there make me think they ain't feed you at all."

Ignoring Marquise as best he could, Keon continued eating at a fast pace. After he finished, he licked the mixture of ketchup and mayonnaise from his hands, balled the tinfoil up, and chucked it out the window.

"Damn, that was good," Keon said, using his tongue to probe around his mouth for meat stuck between his teeth.

Keon pulled the lever on the side of his seat until it reclined in a comfortable position. He closed his eyes and, shortly after, fell asleep.

When Keon awakened an hour later, Marquise was pulling up to the valet in front of the Society Hill Towers on Second and Spruce Streets. They got out of the car and Marquise tossed the keys to the attendant.

"How long you been staying here?" Keon asked, passing the doorman, a tall, husky dark-skinned black

man with big red lips and a cocked left eye. The doorman nodded as he held the door open for the both of
them, and then he closed it just as gently as he opened
it.

"About six months now," Marquise replied, strolling
toward the mailroom to check his box. He pulled out
his BlackBerry and began texting. He continued past
the front desk, making sure to create enough distance
between himself and Keon so that Keon couldn't see
him using the phone.

Keon's eyes lit up and his mouth fell open as he
wandered through the lobby, which was more crowded
than usual due to one elevator being out of service—
something that hardly ever happened. A huge gold
crystal chandelier hung in the center of the lobby. Italian area rugs covered the white marbled floors, which
were so clean that you could see your face in them.

Keon trailed Marquise as they stepped off the elevator and rounded the hallway to his condo, which was
one of three that dominated the floor.

Marquise fumbled in his pocket for his door keys.
When he found them, he unlocked the door and stepped
into the pitch-black apartment.

Keon ducked under the doorway, carefully making
sure not to bump his head, and stepped inside the
apartment.

"Welcome home!" voices yelled in unison.

There were three guys from his old college basketball
team at Villanova lounging on Marquise's ivory-col-
ored Italian leather sectional. Each one had a chick on
his lap wearing nothing more than bikini bottoms and
high heels; their tops lay sprawled across the bamboo
wooden floors.

Keon went down the line, shaking every one of their
hands. He then looked at the women, who were gig-

gling like three little schoolchildren about how gorgeous he was. He rubbed his hands together and then said, "So um . . . which one of you is for me?"

Marquise put his hand around his shoulder and led him away from the pack. "Don't worry about these hoes out here. I got something *real* special for you in here," Marquise said, nodding his head toward the back bedroom.

"Ho? Who you calling a ho?" the light-skinned chick with the long auburn hair asked, folding her arms across her chest.

"You, *ho*. Now shut the fuck up before I kick ya ho ass out," Marquise said over his shoulder.

She rolled her eyes and placed her right hand on her hip, glaring at him in silence.

Turning back to Keon, Marquise guided him down the hall, then knocked softly on the door at the end of the corridor.

"Come in," a sultry voice purred from the other side.

"Go ahead and open the door," Marquise insisted.

Keon grabbed the knob and turned it slightly to the left, cracking the door just enough to peek inside the room. He quickly shut the door just as fast as he opened it.

"Is this some type of joke, man?" Keon asked, whispering as if they were spying on the girls' locker room as they had back in high school. "Is she a man or something? I'm sorry, she look too damn good to be true. Don't fuck wit' me like that, Quise, I'm ready to tear dat ass up something crazy."

Marquise threw his head back and roared with laughter. "Hell naw, that ain't no man. That's Lady Lavender, one of the best bitches in the industry. I paid good money for that ass, now go and tear it up, champ." Marquise patted his shoulder and headed back toward the living room.

Keon delayed his entry even further by wiping his clammy palms on the front of his jeans. He then brushed down his shirt and smelled his armpits to make sure he was still nice and fresh.

"Goddamn, man, just go the hell in there," Marquise yelled, taking a seat beside the same light-skinned chick he cursed out moments before.

Keon slowly opened the door and entered the room, closing the door behind him. He took a seat across from the bed on the cognac-colored leather recliner by the floor-to-ceiling window. The chick's thick, firm thighs lay cocked open, exposing her neatly trimmed kitty. He folded his hands in front of him and watched closely as she penetrated herself with a pink rubber dildo the size of a medium banana in one hand, and rubbed her clit with the other. Her Hershey Chocolate-colored skin wore a slight glow of perspiration, making her look as if she had just dried from the shower. Her jet-black hair lay tidily in a short bob at the back of the nape of her neck, complementing her heart-shaped face. Her eyes were almond shaped and sparkled a shade of honey brown, and her lips were full and pouty, donned with a sheer-nude gloss.

His dick stiffened as her hand left her clit and landed in her moist mouth. His eyes bulged as she sucked on her fingers and placed them back on her clit. She bit her bottom lip and she turned the vibrator up to its maximum setting.

"Are you going to sit there or come join me?" she asked, staring as if she could eat him whole.

"You sure you want me to join you? It looks like you having enough fun over there by yourself," Keon said, slumping down in the recliner.

She turned the dildo off and placed it on the bedside table. Keon's eyes followed her as she got up off the bed and stood before him in her black see-through negligee. Her long dark nipples stood at attention as he grabbed her waist. She ran her tiny hands across his muscular shoulders as she squeezed her curvaceous body between his strapping thighs.

Keon's gigantic hands probed her lower back and then worked their way down to her voluptuous, well-rounded ass.

"You like that, huh?" she asked, jiggling her booty around in his hands.

"Yeah, that's real nice," he said, palming it as if it were a basketball.

"Let's get down to business then," she said, plopping on his lap.

She grabbed at the neck of his T-shirt and ripped it down the center, revealing his toned, well-built chest and perfectly ripped abdomen. His chestnut brown skin appeared flawless at first sight. Her juices flowed as she felt the swollen bulge in his pants extend down to his thigh. Lavender got up from his lap and led him in the direction of the bed. She sat on the side of the bed and patiently waited for him to undress.

Keon kicked off his boots, peeled off his socks, and then lowered his pants to the floor. His six-foot-five frame towered over her as she eased his boxer briefs down to his ankles. Keon watched eagerly as she accepted him in her hot mouth. Her saliva drenched his hardened member as she licked around it like a lollipop. Keon grabbed the back of her neck and forced himself inside her until he could feel the tip of his dick touch her tonsils.

Lavender gagged as he held her head while he came inside her mouth. She swallowed his sperm and licked the leftover secretions from her lips.

Damn, this nigga came quick, she thought, watching as he stepped out of his underwear.

Keon pushed Lavender back on the bed and ripped her negligee from her body just as easy as she had torn his shirt off his. He fondled her perfect C-cup breasts, licking around each nipple and biting softly. He grabbed the black and gold packaged Magnum condom from the nightstand and ripped it open with his teeth. He threw the empty wrapper to the floor and applied the condom with the precision of a doctor, making sure not to rip it in the process. Prying her legs apart like a thief in the night, he thrust himself inside her deep, wet, chocolate walls. His back arched and his muscles flexed as he grabbed the bedpost and dug even deeper into her pussy. He swayed on top of her in short, rhythmic motions.

Lavender's thighs pulsated as he went in and out of her like lightning. In all her days, she'd *never* had a nigga give it to her like this. He didn't want to kiss, or tell her how much he liked her pussy—he just wanted to fuck.

Keon grabbed her petite waist as he felt himself about to cum. Sweat poured from his face onto her stomach, which was also dripping wet from their bodies rubbing up against one another. He grasped her firmly and let out two short pumps. He pulled out, flung the condom off, and covered her chest with his hot liquid.

Lavender licked the cum off her breast. "Damn, that was *good*," she murmured.

"Yeah, same here," Keon said, gathering his clothing from the floor.

Lavender's face balled up as if he just insulted her. Watching closely as he stepped into his underwear and buckled his pants, she realized that he had done to her what she usually did to all her men: kept it straight business. She liked that about him and had to remind herself that it was, indeed, a fuck; something she rarely had to do. He had just the right qualities to become an employee at her establishment.

"So, you just gettin' out the pen, right?" she asked, sitting up on the side of the bed.

"Yup," he said, wondering why she was still talking.

"Do you have a gig lined up? 'Cause I might be able to help you out," she said, reaching under the bed for her purse.

"Oh yeah?" he asked, raising his left eyebrow.

"Just come past my place tomorrow and I'll see what I can do," she said. She opened up her tan Gucci snakeskin clutch with the big G's in the front and returned with a business card.

He looked down at the shiny red card with black engraved letters across the front that read, "The Saddle Club: the premier arena for horseracing." He flipped it over and read the back. He looked back at her and then said, "Lavender Kelley, owner/proprietor. Is this you?"

"Of course it is," she said. She stood up from the bed and picked up her clothes.

"I might just take you up on that offer," he said, and placed the card securely in his back pants pocket.

Keon left the room with what was left of his T-shirt in his hand. When he got to the living room, the same girl who had tried to come at Marquise was now giving him some head on the couch.

Startled by his presence, she jumped up from Marquise's lap and sat beside him.

"What the fuck you stop for?" Marquise asked, pulling her back down to his exposed dick.

She pointed at Keon and said, "Ya boy staring at me."

"Bitch, please, that nigga ain't thinkin' 'bout you. Just keep doing what I'm paying you for."

"Where everybody go?" Keon asked, watching as the redbone went back to work. *She does have a hell of a head game,* Keon thought.

"Them niggas went home to change. We all supposed to meet up tonight at Bleu Martini around eleven."

"Man, I was just going to go to my mom's crib and crash. I don't really feel like going out. Plus, I ain't even got nothing to wear."

"Chill, playboy, I got you. I'm taking care of that as we speak. I sent them other two broads to South Street to pick you up a little something. You gotta hang out. You my nigga. You home and we gonna pick up right back where we left off."

"I can't, man, I got to be in the house by eleven. Remember? I'm on parole."

"Listen, I told you I *got* this. Them parole officers ain't thinking about you. Just come hang with us tonight. We got the whole VIP lounge to ourselves. It's gonna be poppin'. I invited a whole lot of niggas. Now how it's gonna look if you don't show up and it's your party?"

"Okay, okay," Keon said against his better judgment. "I need to get washed up."

"There's some towels in that hallway closet," Marquise said, pushing the girl from his lap and climbing on top of her.

Keon walked back in the direction from which he just came. As he was opening the closet door, Lavender came walking out of the back room with a pair of Seven Skinny jeans, some black open-toed Manolo heels, and a wife beater that was so snug you could see the imprint of her nipples. A waist-length chinchilla coat hung over her right arm.

She threw her tortoise-shell Gucci frames across her face as she walked past Keon and said, "Nice meeting you, babe. I guess I'll see you around."

"Yeah, I guess so," Keon said, drooling as she strutted down the hall and out the apartment door.

Chapter 2

Same Ol' Shit
Keon

It was ten after twelve when they arrived at the club. For a Thursday night, it was crowded like it was the weekend. Keon and Marquise bypassed the line, which nearly wrapped around the block, and were escorted to the VIP section. As they mingled through the crowd, a weird feeling came over Keon: that same feeling he had when he got locked up the first time. He quickly shook it off as paranoia. The security guard lifted the red rope and stepped aside, allowing them into the party. When Marquise passed, he grazed his shoulder and looked him up and down.

"Is there a problem?" Marquise demanded, looking at the security guy through squinted eyes.

"I don't know, you tell me," the short, husky guard said, flexing a tattoo of a pit bull on his forearm with the name "Big Dawg" across it.

"Ain't no problem here," Keon said, stepping in to calm the situation. "We just here to have a good time."

The security officer continued his hard stare in their direction as he hooked the velvet rope closed. Marquise waved a hand in the security guard's direction. "Fuck that nigga, man. He a pussy. He just mad I left with this girl he was trying to get at last time I was here."

"Just relax, man. I can't be going back to jail for no stupid shit. Bad enough I'm out and I shouldn't be."

"Yeah, yeah, you right," Marquise said, changing his tone. "This your night, homie. Ain't nobody is gonna ruin it for you."

Rick Ross's "Hustlin'" thumped throughout the club and his video sprawled across every flat screen in the lounge. Moët bottles lined the tables, as did fresh Cuban cigars. A long, plush red couch aligned the wall in a U-shaped fashion and sheer gold curtains cascaded from the ceiling. Tea light candles flickered around the room, creating just enough brightness to recognize faces. Among them was the chick Lavender he had fucked earlier. She was now dressed in a hot pink miniskirt and a sheer black shirt. Her eyes remained covered but this time with a pair of gold Dior aviator shades. She raised her glass to him and then took a sip. He nodded at her and continued shaking hands around the room.

For once in a long time, Keon felt good. He had all his niggas around him and more pussy than he could shake a stick at. Dressed from head to toe in a pair of black denim Evisu jeans, a sea green button-down Polo shirt, and a pair of fresh Tims on his feet, Keon had all the females looking his way. His reddish brown hair was cut low and his waves were deeper than the ocean. His mustache and beard were trimmed just enough to reveal his baby face. Marquise's barber had come to the crib and tightened him up.

He took a seat in the midst of his old teammates from Villanova; three of them, including Marquise, were all playing in the NBA, two others were playing for foreign teams, overseas. Keon started shying away from the conversation as they began talking about their careers and the money they were making. He sat silently and listened as they compared stories about their teammates. Keon looked around for Marquise; he was over in the corner with three chicks on his heels. He excused himself and strolled over to join the action.

"Sit down, man," Marquise yelled over the music.

Keon sat down beside this thick brown-skinned chick with a wild curly light brown afro and fire engine red lipstick. He smiled at her and she blushed.

"I'll be right back, man. I'ma go see where the fuck the rest of them bottles of Mo at," Marquise said, getting up from the couch and walking off to find a waiter.

Keon nodded and focused his attention back on the female who had crossed her long, slender legs in a way that caused her skirt to rise all the way up near her panty line. Sliding in a little closer, Keon leaned over to whisper something in her ear.

Blam, Blam, Blam, shots rang out in the club, causing everyone to scatter.

Keon jumped up to find out what was going on. He instantly spotted Marquise standing in the middle of the club, waving a Glock in the same guard's face he had words with earlier.

"I keep telling you I ain't no fucking nut," Marquise yelled, letting off two more shots, this time hitting the security guard in his side.

The bullet tore through his flesh, causing him to fall backward. A burning sensation rippled through his body, causing him to shake violently.

Marquise stood over him and aimed the .45 at his head and then said, "Now what, nigga? I should finish you off." Marquise's eyes glazed over as he cocked the gun back for the sixth time and held it sideways.

"What the fuck is wrong with you?" Keon grabbed Marquise by the shoulder.

"Get off of me, man," Marquise said, snatching away from Keon. "This nigga wanted to talk shit so he got dealt with."

"Come on, man, we got to get out of here," Keon pleaded. "I can't go back to jail."

"And let this nigga get away wit' disrespecting me?"

"Fuck that dumb shit, man, you about to fuck up ya whole life."

"What life? Huh, that NBA bullshit. I got cut last season. I just ain't tell nobody. I ain't got shit to lose."

"Nothing to lose? What about your life, your freedom?" Keon's voice trembled.

Hearing the sirens of the cop cars out front, Keon looked around; all of his homies had already taken off out the back door. Before he could make a move, one cop grabbed him by the arm and another had a gun pointed at him.

"Put the gun down," the police officers warned, moving in closer to Marquise with their guns drawn.

Marquise snapped out of his trance and looked around. There were five officers surrounding him. He placed the gun on the floor and put his hands in the air. They quickly cuffed him and led him away.

"I'm sorry, man," Marquise said, turning around to look at Keon.

"Is this one of the ones who was with him?" the tall, pale officer said, pointing at Keon.

"Yeah, that's one of them." The security guard slurred his words. Blood had already soaked through his white T-shirt. He was starting to lose consciousness.

The officer unhooked the cuffs from his belt and placed them around Keon's wrists; they dug into his flesh like a dull knife. Keon held his head low as he was escorted out of the club and into the paddy wagon, a procedure he was all too familiar with. *Here we go again,* he thought, slowly shaking his head as he climbed into the back of the filthy, foul-smelling paddy wagon. *I just went from heaven to hell in one hour.*

Chapter 3

Well Connected
Lavender

The next day when Lavender woke up, her head was throbbing like it was about to explode. She reached from under the covers and felt around on the nightstand until she came across the 225-count bottle of Tylenol she'd bought less than a week ago. She dragged it under the covers and played with the side of the bottle until she felt the two arrows match up. Lavender popped two of the 250-milligrams capsules swiftly in her mouth and swallowed them dry. The average person would have gagged but Lavender was a pro with her mouth. Those little pills were nothing compared to what she was used to putting in it. After fifteen minutes, she pried herself away from her cozy king-sized Sleep Number bed and headed toward the closet. Peeping at the clock on the cable box out of the corner of her eye, she noticed that it was 1:00 P.M. and well past her usual noon start time at work. Thank goodness she owned the place; otherwise, she would have been fired a long time ago. She grabbed the cordless phone from her bedside table and dialed Rafiq's cell phone.

"What's up, Lav," he answered, knowing that she was calling to tell him she was going to be late again.

"Hey, babe, I'm running a little late," she said, grabbing a big, fluffy pea green-colored towel from her closet shelf and continuing toward the bathroom.

He looked up at the clock and then said, "No problem, babe, just get here when you can."

"I'll see you in a few," she said, closing the bathroom door behind her.

"Oh, wait!" Lavender said, screaming into the phone, hoping that he hadn't already hung up.

"Yeah?" Rafiq asked, raising the phone back up to his ear.

"I forgot to tell you that I think I might have found the answer to our little problem with the boys."

"Oh really?" Rafiq said dryly, annoyed that not only was she late to work again, but also making decisions without his input.

"Yeah, I think he'll take us to the next level. I just gotta figure out how to get him out of this jam."

"Here you go again, playing super save a ho." Rafiq said, rolling his eyes as if she could see them on the other side of the phone. "The last time you got someone out of a jam it almost cost us the club."

"Us?" Lavender questioned. "Last time I checked, my name was on the bills there."

"Well, you know what I mean," Rafiq said, wanting to kick himself for what he just said.

Lavender pressed the end button and placed the phone on the toilet seat with her towel. She could tell by Rafiq's tone that he was pissed off but she couldn't care less. He wanted to be a partner and buy into her business but, for now, he was what he was: an employee. Rafiq was a good manager but he was in no way ready to be a partner. He wasn't business minded enough for Lavender.

Lavender turned on the brass spigot with the cream handle and applied the lever to plug the tub. She grabbed the half-empty bottle of Fresh Rice Sake Bath from her shower caddy and poured it in the tub. Lowering her black Hanky Panky chemise to the floor, she turned the spigot to the off position and stepped in the warm water. She slumped back in the tub, hissing as her back hit the cool ceramic. Her head was still aching but not as much as before. She made a mental note to herself to limit her mimosa intake to three a night. She let a little loose in the club last night and wound up having five.

What really was on Lavender's mind was Marquise and his homie getting locked up. She saw it coming so she quickly slipped out of the side door before the cops came. Lavender hadn't known Marquise very long but she did know wherever he went, trouble followed. She really didn't care that Marquise got booked; Lavender was more concerned about his bull. He was just what she needed in order to take her establishment to the next level. He would be a guaranteed star at her club and it had been a long time since she had seen someone like him. Lavender had given him a business card but the look on his face gave her the impression that he just wasn't interested. Her goal was to make sure he came to work for her even if she had to give him a tiny bit of a push.

She shivered as she thought about his thick, lean meat filling her insides like an overripe cucumber. She reached down in between her legs and parted the lips of her pussy like the Red Sea. She stroked her clit like the rightful kitten it was, purring as she felt her juices flow. She then pulled her loofah from the shower caddie and applied L'Occitane Honey and Lemon Foaming Jelly. She began lathering her skin carefully, leaving little white suds circles all over her body. Once she was completely covered she rinsed off and drained the tub. She grabbed the towel from under the phone and patted her body down.

She opened the door to the bathroom, allowing warmness of the bathroom to escape into the cold air. She wrapped the towel around her body as goose bumps burst through her skin. She hurried over to the thermostat in her room and pushed it up to eighty degrees. Lavender hated winter; it always left her skin dry and her nails brittle. As she slathered on Carol's Daughter Almond Cookie Butter from head to toe, it hit her: she would call Benjamin, one of her old clients, to get them off the hook. Benjamin was a municipal judge and had pull. She ran into the living room, almost knocking down the porcelain vase that sat on the espresso-colored hallway table. She fished around her junky Gucci handbag for her BlackBerry and swiftly scrolled through the menu until she reached the phonebook icon. She pressed "B" for Benjamin and pressed talk. Sitting on the side of the bed, she rolled on a pair of black leggings as she waited patiently for him to pick up.

"Hello," a raspy yet proper voice sang into the phone.

Lavender could tell he was back to smoking cigars again. "Hey, Ben, how are you?" She said in her most seductive voice.

"I'm fine, hon. To what do I owe this pleasure?" he asked, lowering his tone to match hers.

"I need a favor," she said, pulling a cream-colored Neiman Marcus sweater dress over her head.

"And what would that be?"

"I need you to get a couple of my friends out of trouble," she said, kneeling down on the floor and searching under the bed for her leopard-print Christian Louboutin booties.

"Send me an e-mail with their information and I'll take care of it. You know you're going to owe me," he whispered.

"Don't I always take care of you?" Lavender said, pulling one of the boots from under the bed and continuing to look for the other.

"So, I'll be hearing from you soon, I presume?" he said.

"Real soon," Lavender said, reaching under the bed as far as she could to grab the other boot, which was in toward the center.

She hung up the phone and swatted at the shoe, moving it closer to her. Grabbing it with the tips of her fingers, Lavender got up from the floor, brushed her sweater down, and shoved on her shoes one after the other.

She applied some lip gloss and a hint of blush to her otherwise unmade-up face and plucked the hairpins out of her bob, which was wrapped neatly against her head. She sashayed to the bathroom mirror and brushed her hair out, allowing it to fall neatly under her chin.

She smiled deviously at herself in the mirror and then said, "Damn, I'm so good-looking it's crazy."

She hurried out to the living room and grabbed her purse and keys from the couch. She grabbed the handle to the front door and, before she could leave, she realized that not only did she forget to e-mail Ben, she forgot her phone. She hustled back to the bedroom, grabbed it from the bed, and began typing the e-mail. She pushed send and made her way back to the living room and out the front door.

Chapter 4

Head Bitch in Charge
Lavender

It was 3:00 P.M. when Lavender pulled up in the parking lot of what seemed like an abandoned warehouse. She got out of her cherry red BMW two-seater and pressed the alarm key. She looked around the other vacant lots that surrounded her and sighed; her location was perfect. Wolf and Swanson Streets were the last places someone would look for an establishment such as hers. It was underdeveloped land and it had been that way for over twenty years. The only other businesses that thrived in the area were the Forman Mills discount clothing store and the auto auction, and that was held twice a week. She threw her bag over her shoulder and pranced over to the red iron door. She rang the bell and looked around the parking lot. There were four cars in the lot: a black BMW 3 series, a silver Jaguar X-Type, a forest green Range Rover Sport, and a gold Maserati Quattroporte. It was a little lighter than usual and this was a problem for Lavender. Her business was still doing well, but after two years of being in service, with the right help, it could be doing a lot better. The exclusivity of the club was one of the reasons why business was slow. Lavender only accepted twenty members at any given time and new spots rarely opened up.

In order to become a member you had to earn at least $500,000 a year. Depending on what you were looking to get into, an hour session could cost you as much as twenty grand. Payment was always made before services were rendered and cash was the only tender allowed. Yes, her prices were steep, but in Lavender's opinion, quality dick never came cheap. One thing she could say about her customers was that they were loyal. The only problem was that they tended to bore easily, so she was always scouting for new talent.

Lavender danced around to keep warm until she heard the bolt on the door click. It was the middle of December and she wouldn't dare put a coat on; it would wrinkle her well put-together outfit. The only time she wore a coat was if it was part of one of her costumes. She would carry one on her arm from time to time as decoration but would never place it on her body.

"Hey, babe," she said, reaching up and planting a big ol' sloppy kiss on Rafiq's cheek as she passed by him.

He wiped at the smeared lip gloss Lavender just left on his face and looked down at his watch. He shook his head and then said, "I swear, you would be late to your own funeral."

"Ha ha ha." She gave off a fake chuckle, opening the counter to the bar.

With her pocketbook still in her arm, she poured herself a stiff glass of Blanton's Single Barrel Bourbon. Besides mimosas and good sex, bourbon was one of her many other guilty pleasures; she enjoyed the taste of a hard, smooth liqueur slithering down her throat. She took another sip and surveyed the club; all five of the forty-two-inch HD flat screens were tuned into different horse races. Ming, her top client, was sitting in the corner on the leather sectional, chatting away on her cell phone. Susan, another big spender, sat opposite of Ming in a leather recliner, puffing on a stogie. She crossed her left leg over her right, causing her black-and-white Kate Spade pencil skirt to rise slightly to her knee.

"So where are all the boys?" she asked, placing the bourbon bottle back on the shelf.

"Well, let's see," Rafiq said, leaning on the bar. "King's upstairs serving a client, and Shane and Tymir should be in the shower; they just finished up a three-way. And the others aren't due until later on."

"Okay, cool," Lavender said, walking from around the bar.

Lavender did the calculations in her head; the boys already made fifteen grand and the club had only been open for three hours.

"I'm looking for that dude I was telling you about to swing past here. Let me know when he arrives; in the meantime, I'll be in my office."

"Okay, but I really don't think we need another body up in here. We doing fine right now."

Lavender placed her right hand on her curvaceous hip and pointed her finger in his face. "First of all, I don't pay you to think. I pay you to do what I say. Secondly, fine is just that: fine. We were bringing in way more money when Vince was here."

"Bitch," Rafiq mumbled quietly under his breath as he turned around and handed her a brown manila envelope with a clasp closure.

She snatched it out of his hand and stuffed it in her bag without so much as saying thank you.

Lavender was growing weary of Rafiq's attitude; he was the reason why Vince was gone anyway. He made poor decisions that almost caused all of them to get caught. She was sick of cleaning up after him and if he made one more mistake she was going to drop him like a bad habit. Rafiq was good at telling other people what to do but at times, he wasn't as good at following directions. She kept him aboard all of this time because she knew him for years; they were both escorts at the same agency. When Lavender decided to branch off and do her own thing, she propositioned Rafiq to join her organization and he accepted her offer.

"Just make sure you let me know when he gets here," she demanded, walking in the direction of the club floor.

She went over to the two clients on the floor and greeted them each separately.

"Hey, Lav," Susan said in a strong Southern accent. A forty-year-old heiress to an oil baron in Texas, Susan moved to Philadelphia to be close to her daughter and grandchild who chose to live a very modest life.

"Susan, babe, how are you?" Lavender asked, lifting her glass to her mouth to take another sip.

"I'm doing good," Susan replied. "But I would be doing much better if you got some new ass in here." Susan flicked the ashes of her heavy burning cigar in the gold ashtray that sat on the table beside her.

"I'm working on it, babe. If things go right I might have something new for you as early as this week."

"I'm going to hold ya to it," Susan said. She took one last puff from the cigar and mashed the stump in the ashtray.

"No problem," Lavender said, heading over to say hello to Ming, who was still yapping away on her phone. Noticing she was in a heated conversation, Lavender just nodded her head to acknowledge her and headed through the back doors and up the stairs to her office. Lavender closed the door and locked it. She then took the envelope from her bag and threw the pocketbook in the bottom left drawer of her desk. She counted the money to make sure it was all there; everything was accounted for. She got on all fours and crawled under her desk. She applied the four-digit code to the safe she kept mounted under it and placed the envelope inside. She got up from the floor and brushed her clothes down. She then pulled out the bottom left hand drawer and grabbed a stack of magazines. She placed them on her desk and begin flipping the pages, overlooking the latest fashion trends as she continued to wait for her guest to arrive. Lavender always stayed up to date on her wardrobe and spared no expense. She folded the edge of the pages where she seen items that she wanted to buy. She looked down at her diamond-encrusted watch that one of her clients bought her several years ago; it was four-fifteen P.M. She couldn't understand for the life of her what was taking so long; usually when she called in a favor, it took less than two hours to have things done. Just as she was looking down at her watch again, the desk phone rang. She waited for the third ring and then answered while continuing to flip through her magazine.

"Good afternoon," she said, already knowing it was Rafiq on the other end. Lavender lived to annoy him and did so every chance she could.

"Your appointment has arrived," he huffed.

"Thank you. Please let him know I'll be right down," she replied, and hung up the phone. She gathered the magazines and stuffed them back in her drawer. Lavender quickly opened the top desk drawer and returned with a small compact mirror. She checked her hair and makeup, placed it back in the drawer, and left the office. When she arrived at the bar to greet Keon, she noticed Rafiq leaning against the bar with his arms folded, pouting like a little baby. She walked right past him without even looking in his direction and greeted her guest.

"Hey, hon, glad to see that you made it," she said, kissing Keon on the cheek. "Let me give you a tour of my spot, and then afterward we can talk business," she said, grabbing his hand and leading him in the direction of the main floor.

"This right here is our lounge area," she said, standing beside Keon with her hands on her hips.

It was after four-thirty and the work crowd was just starting to wander in. There were at least six clients on the floor, sitting around enjoying cocktails, waiting to get serviced. She then led Keon over to the client stairwell. She opened the door and escorted him to the second level. Lavender lagged slightly behind Keon to observe as he explored the staff bathrooms and lounge. Some of the other employees were playing pool and talking shit to each other between clients. She watched as his eyes lit up after he entered room after room.

"So what do you think so far?" Lavender asked, intertwining her arm with his. They continued walking down another short hallway then rounded another long hallway, passing several room doors in the process. The light from three dim wall sconces illuminated the dark corridor.

Keon shrugged his shoulders and then said, "I guess it's cool. But what do I gotta do with all of this?"

"That's exactly what I wanted to talk to you about," Lavender said, rounding the corner and stopping at two wooden doors with gold handles.

She took a single key out of her bag, which dangled from a BMW key chain, and opened the doors. She swung the doors open, revealing a large organized office with a long executive-style desk and a tall leather high-backed chair with steel metal arms. There were papers neatly arranged with paperclips across the desk. A huge lifelike portrait of Lavender sitting naked

Indian style, covering her breasts with her hands hung on the wall above the chair. The walls were painted a fire engine red and draped in gold chiffon fabric. A flat-screen surveillance monitor with twenty-four different camera shots of the club sat across the room above a black metal file cabinet. Leopard-print shag rugs dressed the red birch hardwood floors.

"Have a seat," she said, pointing a sturdy black chair that resembled hers but without the armrest.

Keon sat as instructed and folded his hands in his lap.

"I'ma get straight to the point," Lavender said, walking around her desk to sit down. "I haven't had dick like yours in a long time and I know you'll be an asset around here."

"So what exactly do you do here?" Keon asked, leaning up from his seat. "I mean I have an idea but—"

"Listen," Lavender said, cutting him off. "I just want you to do something that is natural for every man to do: get a nut. I want you to give these women the best fuck of their lives and send them on their way. It's that simple. You've probably been doing it for years but just ain't never get paid to do it. Well, now's your chance."

"So why you want me? I mean you got me out of that shit I got into at the club last night for what?"

Lavender's face lit up as she leaned forward in her seat. "You're just the person I've been looking for. When we fucked yesterday, you didn't catch any feelings. You didn't 'baby this, baby that' me; you gave me the business and put on your clothes and left. That's the kind of qualities I need here at my spot."

"So how does this whole thing work?" Keon asked, shifting around in his seat.

"It works like any other job. You come to work, clock in, do eight hours, and leave. I'll pay you ten dollars an hour on paper and then cut you another forty percent of the money you bring in each week. That way you can stay on the books for your parole officer. So what do you think?"

"Let me think about . . ." Keon said hesitantly. "I really don't want to get into anything that might get me sent back to jail . . . I mean—"

A light knock on the door followed by silence interrupted Keon in the middle of his sentence. Before he could finish, the knock started back up, but this time it was ten times harder than before.

"Are you gonna get that?" Keon asked, looking over at the door.

"Nope," she said, ignoring the knocking and continuing with the conversation. "Think about it?" Lavender asked, sounding confused. "Listen, I can make sure you make more money than you ever seen in your life." She already knew who it was and she wasn't getting out of her seat until Keon signed the contract. She took a blue file folder from her stack of papers and passed it across the desk along with a gold-plated fountain pen.

"A contract though?" Keon said, peering over at the papers on her desk. He was taken aback that she really had legal documents drawn up.

"Hell yeah," Lavender screeched. "I want to make sure that if you try to take me under you're going right along with me. It basically says that you participated in and was a part of this establishment by your own will. That way you'll think twice before trying to turn me in or anybody else that works here."

"You know, you're a piece of work," Keon said, grabbing the pen and the three stapled papers from her hand.

Watching eagerly as he skimmed over the paper, she silently let out a sigh of relief as he sprawled his John

Hancock across the dotted line. Even though her business was illegal, she ran it with the professionalism of a top CEO. Each employee had a file and got paid on the books as bartenders or other domestic help. She paid them a little over minimum wage to insure that they were able to stay legal and on the books with the IRS, child support, or their PO, and the rest was given to them in hard cash.

Lavender snatched the signed document out of his hand and returned it to its original folder.

"See Rafiq on your way out, he'll give you your schedule and answer any other questions you might have," Lavender said, escorting him to the door. "I look forward to doing business with you."

"Yeah, yeah, me too," Keon stammered, opening the door to let himself out.

Lavender closed the door behind him and took a seat back at her desk. She leaned back in her office chair and propped her feet on the desk. With Keon on board, Lavender saw nothing but dollar signs. All she could think about was dollar signs. She knew it was going to take some of the guys time to get used to him but that wasn't her concern. All she cared about was making her clients happy.

It's celebration time, Lavender thought, grabbing her purse from the bottom drawer. She pulled out her wallet and took out a crisp hundred dollar bill and laid it on her desk. She then opened the top right drawer and returned with what looked like a crystallized candy dish. She cleared the papers from in front of her and poured the contents of the dish onto the finished oak wood. Using the edge of the bill, she created four even lines with the precision of an artist at work. She took the hundred dollar bill and rolled it tightly as if she were rolling a joint. Lavender smiled and licked her lips as she leaned over the desk and placed her nose at the top of one of the openings of the bill. She inhaled deeply, allowing the coke to sting her nostrils. Her heart thumped out of her chest as the coke eased its way through her bloodstream. She went to the next line and inhaled again, but this time with the other nostril. A trickle of blood fell over the top, onto the two lines that were left, staining the powder a light red. Lavender grabbed a tissue from the box on her desk and wiped at her nose.

She sat back in her seat and whirled around several times as if she were riding a ride at the amusement park. All of a sudden, she felt hot, sexy, and full of energy; she could use a go around in the sack. She jumped out of her seat and flew around the hallway, leaving her office door wide open and the coke spread across her desk. Hustling down the steps like a masked murderer was after her, Lavender hoped that she could catch Keon before he left.

"Where is he?" she panted, looking frantically at Rafiq.

"He just left out," Rafiq answered, rinsing glasses and placing them on the counter.

She sprinted to the door, causing her four clients on the main floor to stop and look to see what was going on.

"Hey," she yelled across the parking lot.

"What's up?" Keon asked. He placed his hands in his jacket pockets.

She trotted over to him and grabbed his arm. "How about you come back upstairs and give me a little preview of what you going to do in order to keep my clients entertained?"

Keon shook his head and then said, "I don't think that's a good idea. I have to make it home before eight. I don't want my PO trippin' on me."

"Come on," Lavender whined. "Did I mention I was paying?"

Keon's eyebrow rose as he bit down on his bottom lip. "How much?" Keon asked, looking into her eyes and noticing they were somewhat red and glassy. "Never mind, I think I'm just gonna go."

Not taking no for an answer, Lavender stood in front of him and unzipped his dark denim jeans. She slid her hand inside his pants and grabbed his dick through his underwear. It was hard as a rock.

"Either you gonna give it to me or I'ma going to take it. Which one is it?" she asked, massaging him.

Keon pulled her hand out of his pants and zipped them back up. He walked around her and headed back to the door of the club.

"I'm glad you see it my way," Lavender said, smacking him on the ass as she followed him.

Chapter 5

Skimming Off the Top
Rafiq

"Rafiq, right? I was just coming down to see you," Keon said, taking a seat on one of the seven chrome stools that surrounded the bar and folding his hands. "Lavender told me to see you on my way out."

"So you're the new boy, huh," Rafiq said, glancing over at Keon as he continued to dry the glasses at the bar with a green and white checkered dishtowel.

"Yeah, my name is Keon," he said, extending his hand to introduce himself.

Rafiq ignored his gesture and continued wiping down the glasses and placing them on the shelves.

"Listen, Keon," Rafiq grunted with a hint of sarcasm. "In here we don't use government names. That's one of the rules."

"Rules? What rules?" Keon said with a dumbfounded look spread across his face.

Rafiq rolled his eyes in disgust and said, "She didn't explain the rules to you?"

Keon shrugged his shoulders. "Naw, she ain't say nothing 'bout no rules. She just told me to see you."

Rafiq let out a loud groan and tossed the dishtowel on the sink. He walked around the bar and took a seat next to Keon.

"Listen," he said, lowering his voice so only Keon could hear him. "We run a smooth operation here. You come in for ya shifts, do what you gotta do to please the client, and get paid. There are only a few rules that you need to follow and everything else is a breeze; it's a sweet gig."

"So what's the rules?" Keon said, lowering his voice even further to match his.

"First and foremost, never take the client personal. That means no real names, no phone numbers, and no contact outside the club."

Keon nodded his head in agreement. "Cool, I can do that."

"No unprotected sex. We had this one nigga, Vince, who wound up getting two broads pregnant. Man, the shit was crazy as hell," Rafiq said, shaking his head at the drama that unfolded less than six months ago. "On top of getting the chicks knocked up, he tested positive for HIV. On top of that, the dumb nigga fucked around and gave that shit to the mayor's wife. When her husband found out that she was cheating and contracted HIV, it was all over the news. He almost took us all down with his dumb ass. So now we do monthly HIV tests here at the club. And the last rule is real simple: no drug use of any kind."

"So I guess y'all do drug tests, too, huh?" Keon chuckled.

"Yeah, we do," Rafiq said, giving off a stern look. "This may be a joke to you but we take our business seriously and we expect everyone here to do the same."

"So what happens if you break the rules?" Keon stammered through his words with a hint of curiosity in his tone.

"Don't worry about all that. Just do what you gotta and you'll never need to know what happens when you break the rules," Rafiq said, getting up from his barstool. "Since you a newbie, I'll put you on the day shift. That way you can get acquainted with our clientele without feeling overwhelmed. Be here Monday through Friday from eleven A.M. to seven P.M."

"Overwhelmed? Why would I feel overwhelmed?" Keon asked. "I mean all I'm doing is fuckin' them, right?"

Rafiq threw his head back in a light snicker. "Trust me, you can get overwhelmed, especially when more than one client wants you at a time. You have to learn the ropes first."

"So you work too?"

"Naw, I used to but not anymore," Rafiq replied quickly while reestablishing his place on the other side of the bar.

"A'ight then, if that's it, I'm outta here," Keon said, standing up from the barstool.

"See you in the morning," Rafiq said, going back to the task of placing the glasses on the rack.

Rafiq buzzed him out and finished up at the bar. There was something about Keon that made him uneasy. He came across as the typical, cool, down-to-earth type of dude, but Rafiq couldn't shake the feeling that Keon was going to be more drama than a little bit. Rafiq had seen his kind before and knew that he wouldn't last long. That's why he couldn't understand why Lavender was so gung ho about bringing him on. He looked around the club and anger overwhelmed him; he'd practically built that club with Lavender and she still refused to make him a partner. He turned his back to the camera Lavender had positioned in the left corner of the bar and bent down, shielding his hands with his shoulders. He grabbed several twenties out of an old cigar box they used for tips and stuffed them in the front pocket of his shirt.

He then got up and continued wiping the bar down. To Rafiq, skimming a little off the top was something he was accustomed to; it was sort of a bonus for all his hard work that went unnoticed. Lavender was so fucked up off of coke half the time that she didn't know what was going on. Rafiq felt that it was only a matter of time before Lavender would self-destruct and he would be there to pick up the pieces and take over the club. He introduced her to coke a year ago in hopes that she would become addicted and boy was he right. Yes, he snorted with her as well, but only when necessary.

Rafiq chuckled to himself; he felt like an evil villain in a cartoon strip planning his enemy's demise. Lavender was going to give him what he wanted or he was going to take it. With the addition of the new "boy," he could really put some plans into place. He could sense Keon was a gullible, trustworthy type of dude. All he had to do was take him under his wing and everything would come easy after that. He knew that it was only a matter of time before Lavender made him her play toy—she did it to all the guys when they first started.

Chapter 6

Ready for Business
Keon

Keon waited in the darkened parking lot for his cab to arrive. Luckily he did take Lavender up on her offer to make some quick cash; otherwise, he wouldn't have gotten home. A look of relief covered his face as the cab rolled through the parking lot and stopped in front of him.

"Where can I take you?" the cab driver asked, rolling his window down to talk to Keon.

"I'm headed to West Philly," Keon replied, stooping down to peep inside at the driver. "You can let me off at Sixty-third and Malvern."

"Get in," the cab driver said, motioning for Keon to get inside.

Keon opened the door and made himself comfortable in the back seat. He dug into his pocket and pulled out the wad of money that Lavender had just given him. He pulled the rubber band off and chucked it on the floor of the cab. He counted one twenty dollar bill after the other until he was finished; it was a total of $1,000. Keon's eyes grew large as he flipped it over and counted it again. He couldn't believe that he had just made a grand in less than an hour. He placed the money back in his pocket and sat back and closed his eyes. He nodded off as the cab driver weaved through the city to reach his destination.

"Here we are, Sixty-third and Malvern," the cab driver said loudly, pulling over to the curb.

Keon jolted out of his sleep and looked around. He looked at the meter and dug in his pocket to pay the driver.

"Here you go," Keon said, handing him sixty bucks through the Plexiglas window. "Keep the change."

Keon got out of the cab and headed up Malvern Avenue toward his grandmother's house. Keon's footsteps became sluggish as he approached the house adorned with a green and white porch awning. He stopped at the front step and looked up at the wrought iron security door dressed by a wooden wreath with the words "Home Sweet Home" written across it. He grabbed on to the railing and made his way up the steps. He peeped through a small crack in the curtains and saw his grandmother sitting on the couch watching television with her feet propped up on the coffee table. He pressed the bell several times and waited for her to answer.

"Hey, Big Mom," Keon said, peering at his grandmother through the security door.

"Hey, baby," she said, opening the door for him. "I thought you were getting out yesterday."

"I . . . I . . . I was supposed to but there was a mix-up with my paperwork so I had to wait another day to get out," Keon said shakily, avoiding eye contact with his grandmother.

"Is that so," she said, staring into Keon's eyes. "Well anyway, glad you're home, baby."

She embraced him lovingly and kissed him on the cheek. She knew he was lying; she knew her grandson all too well. He only stuttered when he was nervous.

"Come here in the light and let me get a good look at you," she said, walking toward the kitchen, which was brighter than any other room in the house.

Keon stood in front of her and watched as she pushed her glasses up on her nose to get a better look at him.

"You look good, son," his grandmother said, smiling warmly. "I've missed you. I was worried about you in there. You know Big Ma watch them jail shows. I didn't want them boys in there to get to that little tushie of yours."

Keon rolled his eyes and then said, "Come on, Big Ma. You know I wasn't gonna let nobody do nothin' to me."

He kissed her on the cheek and headed straight for the refrigerator as if he'd never left. He flung the door open and stuck his head inside.

"So where's my mom?" Keon asked, returning with a plastic container filled with fried wing dings.

"Aww, baby, I had to put your mom out," Big Ma said, taking a seat at the kitchen table. "She on that stuff again. I came in here one Sunday from church and my new flat-screen TV was gone. You know Big Ma don't play that—I missed a week's worth of *Wheel of Fortune* messin' around with her. She had to go. Last time I saw her she down there on Sixty-second and Lansdowne in front of that ol' bar on the corner. I was riding by on the trolley praying to God she didn't see me."

He shook his head and then said, "Damn, I thought she would have at least got that monkey off her back by now." Keon took a seat beside her, took the top off the container, and started eating it cold.

"Old habits die hard," she said, folding her hands in front of her. "I just hope you keep your nose out of trouble this time around. I can't worry about your momma no more. She love that stuff more than she love me or you. I just gotta let her be."

Keon was having a case of déjà vu; that was the second time he heard that statement within the last forty-eight hours. He didn't care what anyone said about old habits, Keon knew that nothing could ever cause him to go back to jail. He would never be that stupid to get himself into trouble again.

"Yeah, I hear you, Big Ma," Keon said, cleaning the chicken bone and placing it back in the container. "I just wish she would get some help."

"Just pray for her," Big Ma said, patting him on the shoulder as she got up from the table. "Oh yeah, I forgot to tell you that Marquise boy called here for you today. You tell that boy to stop calling here collect. You know I don't answer no collect calls. I wouldn't answer yours; what makes him think I'm going to accept his?"

"Okay, Big Ma, I'll tell him," Keon said, gobbling the remainder of the wing dings down in a matter of minutes.

"I'm going to bed, baby. Your room is just as you left it. Welcome home," she said, smiling at Keon and then proceeding upstairs.

Keon rinsed his bowl out at the sink and placed it in the dish rack. Just as he was turning off the lights downstairs, the phone rang.

"I'll get it," Keon yelled, grasping the receiver of the phone mounted on the kitchen wall. "Hello?"

"Damn, man, it's about time you answered the fuckin' phone. I been calling you all day."

"Yo, Quise, what's up wit' you? How you callin' me, anyway? My big ma was bitchin' about you calling collect."

"I'm using one of the guard's cell phone. But anyway, I don't have much time to holla at you. Looks like I'ma be in here for a minute. I see ya girl Lav got you out. Be careful around her, man."

"Come on with that shit—I ain't worried about that broad," Keon responded, leaning against the refrigerator door.

"You need to be, man, for real. I ain't playing . . . Be careful. I heard a lot of shit about that broad and most of it ain't good."

"I got this," Keon said, turning around to play with the fruit magnets his grandmother had on the refrigerator.

"Yeah, a'ight," Marquise said on the other end. "Don't say I ain't warn you about the bitch."

"Listen, I'ma make sure you taken care of in there," Keon said, ignoring Marquise's concern. "I got you."

"A'ight, homie," Marquise said. "I'ma get at you lata."

Keon hung the phone up and continued through the house turning off all of the lights. *Marquise is worried about me when really he should be worried about himself,* Keon thought as he climbed up the steps to the second floor. Keon opened the door to his room and flicked on the light switch. He smiled as he surveyed the room; it was indeed just as he left it. Posters of Kobe Bryant covered the walls along with several photos of Meagan Good. Countless basketball trophies sat on his dresser, as did a photo of him in his college uniform sporting the number twenty-one. His sneakers were still perfectly aligned at the foot of the bed. Black T-shirt jersey-knit sheets covered his full-sized bed. The Nike duffel bag he used for basketball practice sat in the corner on the red beanbag chair he'd gotten for his twelfth birthday.

He stripped down to his boxers and fell into the bed as if he were at a suite at the Four Seasons. *I'm finally home,* Keon thought, pulling the sheets over his head and closing his eyes.

It was nearly ten-thirty in the morning when Keon arrived for his shift at the club. With a black Nike duffle bag on his shoulder he trudged through the parking lot, leaving the marks of his boot soles on the freshly fallen snow. He took a deep breath as he approached the red metal door, exhaled, and pressed the bell. He then placed his hands back in his pockets and waited for someone to answer. After about ten minutes, Rafiq peeped his head out of the door, looked Keon up and down, and then opened it wide enough so he was able to slide past him and enter the club.

"It's cold as shit out there," Keon said, blowing on his hands to warm them up.

"Didn't you just get home from jail?" Rafiq said smugly, closing the door behind him and planting his butt on a stool in front of the bar. "You should be used to this type of weather."

"Whateva, man," Keon said, trying his best to ignore his remark. "So what you need me to do?"

Rafiq leaned on the bar and took a sip from a can of Red Bull that was in front of him and then said, "First things first, we gotta get you presentable enough for the clients."

"What you mean?" Keon said, finally taking offense to Rafiq and the way he was coming at him. "Presentable?"

"I meant it just like I said it, presentable," Rafiq said with a sly smirk spreading across his face. "See, our clients like their men well-groomed. Nothing against you, but you need a little work in that department."

"Listen, man, you don't know me like that. I'm sick of you smart-ass mouth," Keon said while bubbling inside. "I don't need this shit."

Keon placed his bag back on his shoulder and turned toward the door. He turned the knob and opened it, running right into Lavender, almost knocking her down.

"Where are you going?" Lavender asked, grabbing at her shoulder, which was throbbing from the collision.

"I'm outta here, this nigga be trippin' and shit. I ain't got no time for his smart-ass mouth," Keon said, continuing past her and stepping out in the parking lot.

"Hold on a minute," Lavender said, closing the door slightly to the club to speak with Rafiq.

Keon heard Lavender and Rafiq bickering back and forth; he shook his head and started to walk off. Keon didn't really want to work at the club anyway. He would rather find a job somewhere cleaning floors—real man's work. The money sounded real good to him and he could surely use it to get back on his feet, but he promised himself that he would only work there for six months. That way he could stack his change and start his own cleaning business. Besides basketball, it was the only other thing he was good at.

"Hey!" Lavender yelled from across the parking lot. "Come back inside. I took care of things."

"Naw, I'm good," Keon said, continuing through the parking lot without so much as looking in Lavender's direction.

Lavender followed him through the parking lot and grabbed his arm as soon as he stepped foot on the sidewalk. "I took care of everything," she said, panting heavily. "You won't have any more problems out of Rafiq."

"What the fuck is dude's problem anyway?" Keon asked.

"Rafiq can be an asshole at times," Lavender replied, trying to catch her breath. "He's one of those types of people you either love or hate; there is no in between with him."

"I take it a lot of muthafuckas hate 'em," Keon said. "That little pretty Ricky muthafucka gonna wind up getting hurt."

"Yeah, they do," Lavender said, agreeing with Keon. "He has a habit of saying shit the wrong way. What he meant to say is that we like to make sure our guys are relaxed and well maintained, meaning we have a manicurist, barber, and masseuse on staff. All of our guys meet with them at least once a week."

Lavender led Keon upstairs to the spa area. She flung the door open and revealed a large room with several stations. There was a barber chair, a massage chair, a pedicure chair, and a waxing station placed strategically in the four corners of the room. Jill Scott's "Golden" hummed from the surround-sound speakers.

"Have a seat over there," she said, pointing to the pedicure station. "Huan, our manicurist, will be right with you."

Keon strolled over to the pedicure station and dropped his duffel bag to the floor. He unlaced his boots and peeled off his socks. He shook his head as he rested his feet in the warm basin of water. He felt as though he were selling his soul to the devil. Keon believed in staying groomed, but the whole metrosexual thing just wasn't his thing.

Rafiq appeared at the door just as Huan started working on Keon's feet. With his usual sly grin spread across his face, he watched silently as Keon began his transformation.

"That's right, get down on those feet," Rafiq said, observing the manicurist. "We don't want him tearing up the sheets with those Freddy Krueger toenails of his."

Keon shot him a deadly look. "Quit fuckin' playin' wit' me, man—for real."

Rafiq buckled over in laughter. "Chill out, man, it was just a joke—damn."

"Rafiq," Lavender yelled, looking down at her Black-Berry. "Cut it out."

"Okay, okay, okay," Rafiq said, throwing his hands up in the air. "I'll be downstairs opening the club if you need me."

"No, we won't be needing you. Thank you," Lavender said, looking up from her phone and at Rafiq.

Rafiq disappeared out of the doorway just as he got there.

"I can't stand that dude," Keon confessed. "I swear I'ma wind up hurtin' that nigga."

"I told you don't worry about him," Lavender said. "Just finish up getting ready for today and let me handle Rafiq. Meet me downstairs at the bar when you finished in here."

Keon lay back in the plush pedicure chair and closed his eyes as the manicurist massaged his feet. He had to admit, even though he thought getting pedicures and massages was gay, he did enjoy the pampering. After he was finished with his pedicure he moved to the barber station for a quick shave. Once finished, he noticed a note with his name on it sitting on top of a pair of black D&G boxer briefs, red Polo pajama pants, and a white V-neck T-shirt lying across a black leather chaise longue. On the floor sat a pair of black leather driving moccasins. He lowered his sweatpants and a pair of discolored navy blue Gap boxers to the ground. He then grabbed the boxer briefs and pajama pants and slid them on. He stood in front of a large mirror trimmed in yellow brass and tied the strings of his pants. He pulled the T-shirt over his head and it neatly fell on his body, revealing his well-toned chest and abdomen. His bulging, muscular arms filled the sleeves like it was a second skin. Keon held on to the lounger and slipped one foot after the other into the driving moccasins, which felt so comfortable it was like he was standing on air. He took one last look at himself in the mirror and almost didn't know who he was; he looked like one of those *GQ* model dudes from the magazine. He stroked the hairs of his neatly trimmed facial hair and bit his bottom lip. *Damn, I do look good,* he said to himself. *A nigga could definitely get used to this.* Keon grabbed his things and stuffed them in his duffel bag. He placed it on his shoulder and made his way downstairs to meet Lavender at the bar as she instructed.

Keon stood behind Lavender, who was sitting at the bar chatting away with Rafiq and another tall light-skinned guy with braids. He tapped her on the shoulder and stood back as she swiveled her stool around to see who it was.

"Goddamn, boy!" Lavender shrieked, jumping up from the bar and circling Keon's six-foot-five frame. "You clean up real nice."

She looked over at Rafiq and the other guy she was talking to; they both remained silent while looking him over.

"Let's see . . . What should we call you?" Lavender said, placing her hand on his face and then smacking him playfully. She bit her lip and looked into his huge light brown eyes. "Let's call him Special K."

"Special K?" Rafiq repeated, looking at Keon from across the bar. "I have to admit, I like that."

"Special K it is," Lavender said, walking over to grab her mimosa from the bar. She took a sip and placed it back on the coaster. She took a cigar from her ostrich leather carrying case and cut the tip off. She then lit it and took several puffs back to back.

"It looks like Special K there is ready for business, Lav," Rafiq said, chiming in.

Lavender nodded her head in agreement. She flicked the ashes of the cigar she was smoking into the ashtray on the bar. She sat back down and crossed her legs.

"Now, Special K, I have one question to ask," Lavender said, taking another puff from her cigar and blowing smoke in his face.

"What's that?" Keon asked, swatting at the smoke. Keon wasn't really buying into the whole nickname thing.

"You ready to get this money?" Lavender asked, as if she was his pimp and he was on the stroll.

Chapter 7

Working Man
Keon

"It's time to get to work. Room 200 is yours. So, go get ready, I'll be sending a client up shortly," Lavender said, placing a single gold key in the palm of Keon's hand.

"A'ight," Keon said, heading for the stairs.

His hands clammed up as he approached the flat-paneled oak door to the room. He placed the key in the lock and turned the knob. Keon laid eyes upon a luxurious king-sized bed draped in black-and-white zebra-print sheets. Over the bed hung a wrought iron chandelier accented with crystals; black handmade Persian rugs covered the wooden floors. Candlelit wall sconces illuminated the room. Nightstands with Magnum condoms and cans of Red Bull sat on both sides of the bed. He walked in and as he tried to close the door behind him, a small, dainty hand covered with henna grabbed it to keep it open. Keon looked behind him and there stood a petite Indian woman dressed in traditional garb. A red bindi mark lay between her eyebrows and a small gold ring decorated her nose.

"Hey, how you doin'?" Keon asked, giving off a fake smile.

Keon glanced at her face. She was a middle-aged woman with dark almond-shaped eyes, and full, pouty lips. She wasn't bad looking, she just wasn't exactly what he envisioned as his first client, but he knew he would just have to run with it. He hoped he was able to get a hard-on and that his dick didn't let him down.

"Hello to you," she said, closing the door and pushing him toward the bed.

"So, what's your name? That is, if you don't mind me asking," Keon said.

"My name is Raji," she said, stepping out of her shoes.

Keon watched as she carefully undressed, revealing a round, supple ass, breasts the size of small honeydew melons, and the curviest hips he'd ever seen; they reminded him of the shape of a Coke bottle. Keon's dick hardened as she unpinned her bun and her long dark brown hair fell well past her shoulders, slightly covering her nipples. He grabbed at his bulge in his crotch as she stood before him naked with gold bangles dangling from both wrists.

"Here, let me help you with that," she said, climbing on top of his tall, muscular frame and untying his pajama pants.

Keon brushed the hair out of her face and pulled her close to him. He kissed her lips several times and then slithered his hot, moist tongue in and out of her mouth. He pinched at her large brown nipples, which were at full erection. He grasped her hips and made his way down to her round ass. He smacked it once, leaving a red hand mark on her right cheek.

"Eat my pussy," she demanded, feeling at the oversized swelling in his pants.

Keon traced her lips with his tongue and flipped her over off of him and on her back. He hovered over her as if she were his prey and kissed her fervently on the lips. He reached down in between her thighs and massaged her clit with his index finger. He bit and sucked on her nipple, causing her to moan lightly.

"Eat my pussy," she demanded again, grabbing at his head and pushing it downward.

Keon snatched her hand away and pinned it down with his. His tongue continued to explore her body, leaving her chest, gliding down to her stomach and as he approached her thighs, he tore them apart as wide as they would go and bit at the hood of her vagina. Keon twirled his tongue around on her clit while slurping up all of her juices.

"*Yes,*" she hissed, clawing at the sheets surrounding her. "Just like that."

Keon stood up, grabbed her waist, and forcefully pulled her body toward the edge of the bed. He got on his knees and burrowed his head deep into her pussy. He used his middle finger to penetrate her as he continued biting and sucking on her. Her juices flowed down his face as he hummed between her thighs, giving off a subtle yet powerful vibration to her clitoris.

"Fuck me," she yelled, panting heavily.

Keon got up off his knees, went around to the side of the bed and grabbed a Magnum condom from the nightstand. He ripped the package open with his teeth and placed it on his dick, making sure there was enough room at the top to catch his liquids. He then got on top of her and spread her legs apart. He grabbed a fistful of her hair in one hand and entered inside her juicy walls, stroking her like a man possessed. Thrusting back and forth in long, rhythmic motions, Keon gripped her hair tighter, pulling her face toward him. He continued to caress her tongue with his stopping here and there only so she was able to catch her breath.

"Oh God!" she screamed, scratching his back as he picked up the pace using short, circular motions.

"Whose pussy is this?" he asked, lifting her legs toward to ceiling, digging deeper into her tight, wet walls.

"Yours, baby," she shouted, holding her legs up with her hands. "It's your pussy."

Raji's body quivered as he pulled his dick all the way out and drove back into her pussy. Sweat poured from his arms and chest, moistening Raji's body in the process.

"Turn around," Keon demanded, pulling out of her pussy and inspecting the condom to make sure it was still intact.

She got on all fours with her ass up in the air and buried her head in the pillow.

Keon carefully guided himself back into her pussy, gripping her waist with one hand and her hair with the other. Keon yanked her up from the pillow and pounded her petite frame into his like a crazed madman.

"Oh shit, oh shit, oh shit," she said, holding on to the end of the mattress as he continued picking up the pace. "I'm about to cum."

Keon let go of her hair and wrapped his hand around her body. He opened the lips to her vagina and fingered her all while continuing to stroke her warm, ripe pussy.

"Let that shit out," he whispered. "Go 'head, come for daddy."

"Oh God!" Raji shrieked. "I'm coming!"

Her eyes teared as she erupted from pure pleasure. She had had many orgasms before but never at the level that she had just experienced. She couldn't stop her body from shivering.

Keon jumped up from the bed, peeled the condom off of his still fully erect dick, and dropped it in the wastebasket. He made his way to the bathroom, turned on the shower and got in. He used a bar of Irish Springs and lathered his body from head to toe. He quickly

rinsed off and grabbed his towel from the rack behind
the door. He toweled off and stepped back into his
room. He looked over at Raji, she was still trying to
gather herself from the wild sex they just had. Her hair
was all over the place from him pulling on it. He stood
by the dresser as he watched her put on her clothes and
brush her hair back in a unruly ponytail. He continued
staring at her as she put her loosely fitting clothes back
on, covering her shapely body. Keon placed his arms
around her neck and kissed her on the forehead. He
then grabbed the door knob and stood to the side to let
Raji out.

When Keon opened the door to the room, three of
the other guys on duty were hovering around the door,
whispering. He excused himself and they all fell quiet
and moved to the side to let him past. Keon guided Raji
down the hallway to the client's restroom. Keon's face
wore a cocky smirk as he cruised through the hallway.
He knew that they heard her in there screaming at the
top of her lungs, asking for God to have mercy on her.
He already had it in his mind that he wouldn't become
cool with anyone. All he wanted to do was do his job,
and go home. He didn't care that they were whispering
about him. Keon already knew that they looked at him
as a threat; he could tell by how they looked him up and
down as he left. He nodded goodbye and started back
in the direction in which he just came.

"I'll see you again next week," Raji yelled, holding
the door open to the restroom.

Keon turned around and then said, "Same time?"

"Same time," she repeated, blushing from ear to ear..

When Keon got downstairs, there were several other
clients sitting around, waiting to get serviced. He was
actually hoping that he would have another rendezvous. Keon had a very high sex drive and even though

he enjoyed his session with Raji, he didn't get his shit
off.

"Let me get a shot of Henny," he said, taking a seat
next to Lavender at the bar.

"So . . . how was it?" Lavender asked, handing him a
cigar. "You know you just made five grand, right?" She
lit it for him and eagerly awaited his response.

"Not bad at all," Keon responded, blowing out a big
cloud of smoke. "Not bad at all."

Chapter 8

Living With Regrets
Keon

At the end of his shift, Keon changed back into his street clothes and prepared to head home for the night. It was close to eight P.M. when he left the club. He listened to his earphones as he waited for the bus to arrive. Once on board, he took a seat in the very back by the window. He nodded on and off for an hour before he reached his destination. He then got off the bus at Fifty-sixth Street and Lansdowne Avenue and headed toward the bar on the corner of Sixty-second Street. He knew that he was in violation of his parole but after the day he had, he needed to unwind and it was the only place he could think of at the time.

With his Nike duffel on his shoulder, Keon opened the smoked out door to the bar and went in. It was fairly quiet with only a handful of patrons inside. The jukebox cranked out the sounds of The Whisper's Rock Steady and a middle-aged woman stood in the middle of the floor dancing and snapping her fingers while lip synching the words. Keon took a seat toward the front of the bar by the door. He dropped his bag to the floor and placed his jacket on the back of his chair. He put a twenty dollar bill on the bar and waited to be serviced. The bar tender; a tall, thick brown skin young girl appeared in front of him, ready to take his order.

"Can I get a Hennessy and Coke," Keon asked, pushing the twenty in her direction without looking at her. He was too busy looking at the television above the bar; the Eagles game was on and they were getting blown out by the Pittsburgh Steelers.

"Keon, is that you?" A familiar voice asked.

Keon's attention was quickly pulled away from the television and refocused on the woman standing in front of him. "Chevy? Damn baby, I ain't know that was you. How you been?" Keon reached over the bar and hugged her. The smell of Bath and Body Works Midnight Pomegranate filled his nostrils. The familiar scent caused his dick to stand at attention. He quickly thought about something unrelated to sex so that he could calm himself down. Chevy was actually the last chick he was seeing before he got locked up; they were together for a year. She had came and seen him a few times while he was in prison but after two months or so, she faded off and he never heard from her again. He sat back down in his seat and continued to look her over. Her hair was dyed a shade of bright red and fell effortlessly on her shoulders in cascading curls. A pair of black tights hugged her hips and thighs. A black baby doll t-shirt with the word Sexy written on it covered her large breasts. Her face was made-up as if she was going to a photo shoot. Light pink gloss stained her lips and shades of brown and gold eye shadow covered her lids. Large hoops hung from her ears and her right arms were covered with silver bangles.

"I been good," She said, leaning on the bar. "How have you been?"

"I'm cool. I just got out the other day." Keon said, continuing to look her up and down. He couldn't help but to stare at her. She was only eighteen when he got locked up and even though for the most part she looked the same, she seemed to have matured a lot. He wanted to ask her why she stopped writing and coming to see him but he played it cool; he didn't want to come off as bitter.

"That's what's up? So what you gonna do now?" She asked, turning her back as she poured his drink.

"I found myself a gig at this building downtown doing janitorial work," Keon said, folding his hands in front of him on the bar. "How long you been working here?"

"I just started last week," Chevy said, placing the drink on a coaster in front of him. "I'm in hair school during the day and I come here afterwards."

"Hair school—that's what's up," Keon said, taking a sip from his glass. Keon was digging the fact that she didn't end up like the rest of the girls in the neighborhood and that she decided to do something with herself. Keon drowned the rest of his drink and motioned for her to make him another. He watched her ass jiggle as she turned away from him and reached up on the shelf to grab another glass. His dick hardened for a second time as he visualized himself grabbing her by the waist and grinding her plump round ass.

"Here you go," Chevy said, placing another drink in front of him. She smiled and cut her eyes at him as she rushed to the other end of the bar to take another order.

Keon turned his attention back to the game and continued to sip on his drink. He continued to peep out of the corner of his eye as she rushed up and down the bar making drinks. Keon looked down at his watch; it was almost eleven and he needed to make it in the house before his parole officer called at midnight. He finished his drink and left the remainder of the twenty dollars on the bar for a tip. He got up from the chair and threw his coat on. He grabbed his bag from the floor and placed it on his shoulder. He then nodded at Chevy to let her know that he was leaving out.

She dropped the wash rag in the sink and rushed over to where he was. "I'm about to get off at any minute now. Why don't you come over my house so we can catch up?" Chevy said, biting her bottom lip to let him know what it was really hitting for.

"You still live up the street wit your peoples?" Keon asked, taking a seat back at the bar.

"Yeah, yeah I still live with them," she said. "It'll be like old times. I can sneak you in through the back door."

Keon let out a soft chuckle as he thought about how many times he came through the alley to get in the house when her mother went to sleep at night. "Aight cool, let me know when you ready." Keon dropped his bag back on the floor. Just as he was getting back to the game which was now in overtime, Chevy was tapping him on the shoulder. He turned around on the stool he was sitting on. "You sure you wanna hang wit me?" Keon asked, licking his lips and looking at her as if she was a piece of meat.

"Would you come on boy and stop playin," Chevy said, pulling his hand. "I'm a grown ass woman, I got this." She turned toward the door and went outside.

Keon grabbed his bag and quickly followed behind her. They remained silent as they walked down the street to her house. Keon had many questions that he wanted to ask her but he decided that he was going to enjoy whatever came out of their little rendezvous instead of making it serious. He still had serious feelings for Chevy and thought about her often. He was the first guy she ever had sex with and in Keon's mind, he knew that he would always have a special place in her heart.

"Wait here," Chevy said when they arrived at the house.

Keon stood over by the light pole as instructed and watched as she ran up the steps and opened the door to the house.

"It's clear, I'll meet you at the back door," Chevy said, disappearing in the house.

Keon started down the dark alley, counting houses to make sure he ended up at the right place. The neighbor's dog barked viciously as he opened the gate to the yard causing Keon to rush up the steps and inside the door. He'd never got caught sneaking into Chevy's house before and he wasn't trying to get caught now. He dropped his bag as well as his coat in the shed and locked the back door. Chevy was standing in the kitchen door waiting for him.

Keon pressed her body against the door frame leaving no space for her to move. "You miss me?" he asked pushing her hair aside and cupping her face in his gigantic hands.

"I missed you so much," Chevy whispered, grabbing his face with her baby soft hands."I'm so sorry for . . ."

Keon pressed his lips against hers, stealing her breath away in the middle of her sentence. He grabbed her hands away from his face and pinned them up against the wall with his as he continued to probe her mouth with his hot, wet tongue. He stopped for a second to catch his breath and went right back to her soft succulent lips, sucking on them as if they were a piece of hard candy. He backed away and listened to the sound of her heart pounding as they stood in complete darkness.

"I love you, Keon," Chevy blurted out, burying her head in his chest.

"I love you too," Keon responded, surprised with himself that he was actually able to tell her how he felt. Back in the day when they were together, she would ask him did he love her and he would never respond. He wrapped his arms around her as tight as he could, wishing he could get back all of the time he missed being without her. "Come on," he took her hand led her toward the door to the basement where her room was located. He flicked on the light and ducked down as low as he could so he wouldn't bump his head as he crept down the steep steps.

Chevy stood at the bottom of the basement steps and pulled her shirt over her head and tossed it over in a pile of clothes. She then peeled the black tights from her body and tossed them in the same direction.

Keon wrestled with the buckle on his jeans as she unhooked the clasp on her lace, turquoise blue bra. He pushed his pants around his ankles and stepped out of them as he continued to watch her take off a matching pair of boy shorts. Keon couldn't control himself any longer. He shoved his boxer briefs to the floor, revealing his full erection. He pulled at it, stroking it with care as Chevy made her way across the room toward the bed where he was now sitting.

"So you did miss me," Chevy joked, taking his hardened member in her hand and continuing to stroke it where Keon left off.

"What you think?" He asked, smacking her hard on the ass.

"I'll take that as a yes," she said, pushing him back on the bed.

She climbed on top of him and kissed him sweetly on the lips while continuing to play with his hardened member. As their kisses got more intense, she slid his rod inside her warm walls.

"Wait," Keon said inbetween kisses. "You ain't gonna use no condom?"

"For what?" Chevy said. " I ain't been fuckin nobody and I'm on the pill."

"I still think we should use one." Keon said, trying to not allow his eyes to roll back into his head as she gyrated her hips around on him as if she was a professional porn star.

"Would you just chill and enjoy this good pussy," Chevy purred, bouncing up and down on him like a jack rabbit.

Keon bit his bottom lip as she tightened her kegal mucle and squirted her juices all over him. He was no longer concerned about a condom, he was so turned out that he came two times back to back and got hard again within seconds. Despite the incident that happened at the club with Marquis, Keon was starting to think that he was lucky dude. He had more pussy in the last forty-right hours that he had in his entire life. He closed his eyes and allowed her to take control of his body. He couldn't help but to moan, not only was the sex good but he loved her so that made it even better. He grabbed her by the neck and squeezed it lightly as he felt himself about to erupt for a third time.

She covered his mouth with her hand to muffle his moans which were starting to get louder as he slipped into ecstasy.

"Mommy," a little voice squealed. "Where are you?"

Chevy thought she was hearing things at first so she continued riding Keon as if she was a cowgirl in the rodeo. She threw her head back, closed her eyes and she heard the little voice again.

"Mommy, I'm scared," the little voiced squealed again.

Chevy's body came to an abrupt stop as she realized who it was.

"Down here baby," Chevy responded, leaving Keon's warm embrace to grab her bathrobe to cover her naked body She tossed the sheet which had fallen on the floor during their love making over Keon's bare body; leaving nothing revealed but his feet. She went over to the steps and stood there as she watched her daughter take one step at a time to get to her. She grabbed her from the last step and brought her over to the bed where Keon was still lying.

"Hey, I didn't know you had a kid," Keon said, pulling the sheet closer to his body. He felt somewhat uncomfortable that Chevy was allowing her daughter to come downstairs in the middle of them getting it on.

Chevy sat on the side of the bed and hoisted the little girl up on her lap. She wrapped her arms around the little girl and hugged her tightly. She then let out a loud sigh and then said, "Keon, *we* have a daughter."

"We?" Keon said looking very confused. "What do you mean we?"

"Mariah is your daughter—Keon," Chevy said, looking over at him with sad eyes. "When you got locked up I was pregnant. I didn't find out until I was almost four months. When they told me I was pregnant I went from loving you to hating you because I knew that you were gone and that you wouldn't be in my life or hers."

"So is that why you stop writing me and coming to see me?" Keon asked, looking at her and then at the little girl who was now playing with her mommy's finger nails.

"Yeah," Chevy mumbled with her head down.

Keon sat up from the bed, making sure that his body was still fully covered and inched over by where Chevy was sitting. He put his arm around her and pulled her close. He kissed her on the cheek and then said, "Everything is going to be okay . . . I promise." Keon's mind raced as he tried to consume the notion of having a child. He never in a million years thought that this was the reason why Chevy just up and left him alone. In Keon's book, having a child was a huge responsibility and he wasn't sure if he was ready to be a father. He knew he didn't have too much of a choice but he was definitely frightened that he wouldn't be a good one. He never met his father and vowed that he never wanted to have children because he didn't want to ever be like his or any other man that wasn't around for their kids. He already had regrets about being locked up when she was born. He rubbed her shoulders as he tried to ease his own mind. He couldn't help but to steal an up close look at the little girl. When he looked into her eyes; he saw a picture of himself. She had all of his keen features from his large brown eyes to his short wide nose. Keon did the calculations in his head, if he was right she should be two and a half years old.

"I'm sorry you had to find out like this. I tried to write you over and over to tell you but I just didn't know how. Every time I started to write you I wound up tearing the letter up," Chevy's eyes started to tear up. "She's such a sweet little Girl, K. She has your crazy laugh and she loves to dance and act silly just like you."

"I'm going to be there for her. I know I might have not been there in the past but I swear I'm going to be there for her and be the best father I can be." Keon said, squeezing Chevy tightly.

"I'll be right back," Chevy said getting up from the bed with the baby in her arms. "I'm going to put her back to sleep."

"Aight," Keon said leaning back on the bed.

Chevy disappeared upstairs and returned within minutes. She stripped out of her bathrobe and climbed over Keon's body to the other side of the bed. He grabbed her close to him; the sound of her heartbeat soothed him as it did when they were together. Before he knew it; he had nodded off and was fast asleep.

Keon jumped up from the bed and looked at the clock on the cable box in Chevy's room; it read three am. "Shit," Keon cursed, scrambling to find his clothes. He knew that he was in deep trouble; he'd missed his PO's phone call for sure. He tossed on his jeans, not even stopping to find his underwear. He threw on his shirt and stepped into his boots. Keon kissed Chevy on the head and headed for the steps.

"Where are you going?" Chevy asked, half sleep.

"I gotta go home. If I'm not working, I have to be in the house by midnight. I'm praying to God I don't get locked back up for this shit."

"Wait," Chevy said, stopping him at the steps. "When am I . . . I mean Mariah going to see you again."

"Don't worry, I'll be in touch. I'm staying at my grandma house anyway so you know where to find me." Keon said, starting up the steps to the basement. He grabbed his coat and duffel from the shed and started out the back door. He hustled through the alley with his hands in his pocket. The cool December winds cut at his exposed face as he exited the alley on the side street and started home. Keon continued to think about his daughter as he walked briskly through the vacant streets. He also thought about the possibility of him and Chevy getting back together. As Keon approached his block, he slowed up and paid close attention to his surroundings. He knew that there a possibility that his PO had sent officers out to get him. He walked in the shadows of the trees until he reached the house. He had his key already ready to open the door so he took a deep breath and ran up the steps taking two at a time until he reached the porch. He quickly unlocked the door and went inside.

Keon could tell from the darkened house that his grandmother hadn't realized that he didn't make it home on time because if she did, she would have been sitting up waiting for him to come with her bible in her lap. Keon hurried over to the phone to check the caller ID; it was lit up with over ten calls from his PO. Keon's stomach turned sour as he thought about the possibility of going back to jail. He quickly searched his jacket pocket for Lavender's card and dialed her cell phone. He left her a quick message to let her know what was going on in hopes that she would be able to pull a few strings for him. He then made his way upstairs to his room, making sure he didn't make any unnecessary noise that would wake his grandmother up. The last thing he needed was a lecture about coming in late. He laid across the bed with his clothes on, thinking about Chevy and Mariah. Before he knew it; he was sleep.

Chapter 9

The Clash of the Titans
Rafiq

"Your PO just left here," Rafiq said, handing Keon an envelope full of cash from his earnings last week. "He wanted to know how you was doing at work."

"Oh yeah?" Keon chuckled, grabbing the envelope and stuffing it in his jacket pocket. "And what did you tell him?"

Rafiq grinned and then said, "I told him that you was my best employee. And that you did your job with diligence and ease." Both Rafiq and Keon doubled over with laughter.

"Good lookin'," Keon said, giving him a pound. "That dude been on my back lately. All because I missed his phone call the other night. I told him I was at work that day and I got off late."

"Yeah, he asked about that too," Rafiq said. "I told him that you got caught up waxing." They burst out laughing again.

"Yeah, I was waxing—waxing Daisy's ass like a fuckin' monster. She was screaming so fuckin' loud that Lav had to come knock on the door and ask her to keep it down. Where is Lav anyway? I ain't seen here in a whole minute," Keon asked.

"She had some personal business to take care of," Rafiq said, looking down at his watch. "She should be in today though, in about an hour or so."

Rafiq was tired of covering for her ass when the boys asked where she was. He had no other choice. If they knew she was coked up half the time they would lose respect for her and thus the club in general. Rafiq couldn't allow that to happen because then they would think that it was sweet around there and start doing whatever they wanted. So he kept things running smoothly, and made sure all the guys were paid on time and that the clients were always happy.

"Cool," Keon said, surveying the club. "I see Kathy over there; is she my first appointment today?"

"Yup," Rafiq said, handing Keon a can of Red Bull. "You're gonna need this."

"True, true," Keon said, popping the top open. "Let me get up here and get ready for business."

"I'll send her up in like fifteen minutes or so," Rafiq said, handing him another Red Bull. "You gonna need this—afterward. We all know Kathy is an old cougar." They both nodded at each other and Keon disappeared up the steps.

Rafiq observed the main floor as he sat down at the bar and popped open a Heineken; there were eight members there and it was just turning two P.M. Rafiq had to admit, the club had been booming ever since Keon came on. He knew he was against it from the beginning, but it was actually the best idea she'd had in a long time. It was so busy lately that most of the guys had been working double shifts. The clients seemed extremely happy with the type of care and attention Keon gave them during their sessions, so much so that his appointment book always remained full. He caused a lot of the other guys to have to step their game up in the bedroom and, in turn, their books were also full. Rafiq figured that if they could just accept five new members and keep the momentum up with the boys, everyone in the club including himself would be sitting pretty. That meant that there would be a total of twenty-five women who had access to the club and, if Rafiq's calculations were right, there was a possibility to bring in an extra thirty grand a month.

He planned on talking to Lavender about taking in new clients but, lately, she'd been so high that the only time she came to work was to get money to feed her habit and then out the door she went. This was his twelfth day straight, opening and closing the club. That's exactly why he was ready to have a sit-down with her and ask her to allow him to take over things and make him partner. He deserved it; she never did any work anyway. He knew for sure that she would love the idea of taking on a few new members because it would bring in more cash and, if he knew anything about Lavender, he knew that she was all about her dough. Well, when she wasn't spending it on coke that is.

Plus, Rafiq needed more money—period. Yes, he skimmed off the top here and there but he needed a real raise. His baby girl was starting college next fall and he wanted to make sure she was taken care of. He had a set of twins in private school and his wife wanted a new house. He knew he would make more money if he started working again but he promised his wife his days of having sex for money were over, and he knew if she found out he was even considering it, she would leave his ass high and dry. It was a chance he just wasn't ready to take.

"Hey, honey," Ming said, sliding onto a stool next to Rafiq. "Let me get a glass of chardonnay."

She dumped her red Balenciaga bag and black Dior sunglasses on the bar and pulled out her compact. She powdered her nose and took another look at her freshly cut, shoulder-length bob.

"Sure, babe, no problem," Rafiq said, jumping up from the stool and returning to his proper place behind the bar.

He grabbed a wineglass from the rack and prepared the drink. Ming was one of Rafiq's favorite clients. She spent a lot of money in the club and she was a regular. You saw her at least once a week, whereas some of their members only showed up once or twice a month.

He placed it on a coaster in front of her and smiled brightly. "So what brings you here today?"

"Does Special K have any openings?" Ming asked, taking a sip from the glass. "I figured if I got here early, you could maybe squeeze me in." She gave off a smile and continued sipping from her drink.

Rafiq dipped under the counter and returned with the appointment book. He flipped through several pages until he came to today's date.

"Let's see, today is Wednesday, March third," Rafiq said, using his finger to skim Keon's appointments for the day. "I'm sorry, baby, he's booked solid until he leaves tonight."

"Are you sure?" Ming asked, sliding a folded-up one hundred dollar bill under her now empty glass and pushing it in Rafiq's direction.

Rafiq looked at the book again. "I think I see an opening here at four. Why don't I just pencil you in right here?"

"Thanks, darling," Ming said, leaning over and kissing Rafiq on the cheek. "I'll be right over there," she said, pointing in the direction of the main floor.

"No problem," Rafiq said, clearing her glass from the bar and stuffing the bill into his jeans pocket. "I'll call you when you're up."

Ming nodded and grabbed her bag from the bar. She headed in the direction of the main floor and took a seat in the corner on the recliner as she always did when waiting to be serviced.

Meanwhile, Rafiq continued with his daily duties. Once the bar was cleaned and restocked, he started the daily paperwork including the money count. He squatted down, pressed in the six-digit code to the safe, and started counting; there was a total of fifty grand there, including twenty grand from the previous night. He checked his records again; there was five grand missing. He quickly placed the cash back in the safe and locked it. He dug in his pocket for his cell phone and dialed Lavender's cell phone; it went straight to voice mail. He knew she must have come in last night after the club closed and hit the safe up. Rafiq couldn't wait until she came in the club. He was going to give her an ultimatum: either make him partner, or he was going to quit. She couldn't possibly run the club by herself; it would crash and burn within a matter of a month. He logged the numbers in the paperwork and placed the accounting log back on top of the safe.

It was close to midnight when the doorbell began ringing uncontrollably; he knew that it was no one but Lavender. She was the only person who acted as if they couldn't wait to be let in. When he spoke with her that morning, she said she would be in around four or five in the afternoon, and now she wanted everyone to stop what they were doing to tend to her foolishness. He was hoping to have the conversation with her earlier but he had no choice but to speak to her about it tonight. Rafiq took a deep breath and exhaled, threw his dishtowel in the sink, and headed over to the door to answer. He peered through the peephole, and standing there in pure darkness with a pair of Dior aviator shades covering her face was Lavender. He opened the door and she brushed past him and headed straight to the bar to fix a drink.

"Hello to you too," Rafiq said, looking her over.

Her china doll wig was all out of place; stray hairs covered her face. Her lips were stained with red lipstick and her nail polish was chipped; she was in desperate need of a manicure. Rafiq shook his head as he watched her down two shot glasses of bourbon as if it were spring water.

"So where you been?" Rafiq asked, wiping down the counter where she just spilled half a cup of bourbon pouring herself a shot.

Lavender shot him a dirty look. "When did you become my father?"

"The boys been asking me where you been, rather," Rafiq said, trying his best to rephrase his last statement.

"They been getting paid, right?" Lavender asked, pushing the shot glass to the side and sipping out of the bottle.

"Yeah, they been getting paid," Rafiq confirmed.

"That's all they need to worry about," Lavender said, finishing off the rest of the bourbon and tossing the bottle in the trash can.

Rafiq watched as she placed her sunglasses on top of her head and bent down to open the safe. He stood over her and then said, "Did you take some money out the safe last night?"

"Yeah, I did," Lavender confirmed. "I had to take care of some business," she said, pressing in the code and counting off what looked like seven grand. She closed the safe and stuffed the money in her bra.

"Sure you did," Rafiq blurted out without even thinking.

"What the fuck is that supposed to mean?" Lavender asked, sucking her teeth. "It's my fuckin' club and I'll do what I damn well please."

His face turned bright red and his skin grew hot as he fought the urge to slap the bullshit out of her. "I need to talk to you about just that," Rafiq said, gritting his teeth. "I've been working my ass off in this club, opening and closing day after day. I think it's time that you really consider making me a partner."

"Ha!" Lavender said, chuckling as if he were some sort of comedian. "Naw, you ain't ready for that type of responsibility."

"What the fuck do you mean, I'm not ready for that type of responsibility," Rafiq said, moving closer in Lavender's direction with his fists balled at his sides. "I work my ass off in this place," Rafiq yelled, pointing his finger in her face.

"Whateva, Rafiq. You always around here acting like you're running shit. But your attitude is shitty. You play favorites with the boys and the customers complain about you watering down the drinks. And don't think I don't know you been taking money on the side to fit people in. Just because I'm not here doesn't mean I don't know what's going on at my establishment. You've been skimming money off the top for years, and I never mentioned it. I just let you do what you do. You're just not partner material," Lavender said, placing her hand on her hip. "So stop asking me."

When Rafiq realized it, they were so close that he could smell the alcohol seeping out of her pores. He peered into her eyes; they were stone red and glassy. Before he knew it, he had his hands wrapped around her neck so tight that her eyes bulged and her dark brown skin turned red.

"You pussy," Lavender coughed, massaging her neck. "I'm gonna fuckin' kill you." Lavender rushed over to her satchel and dug through it like a madwoman.

Rafiq knew Lavender kept a little pocket-sized .22 in her purse. "I'm sorry," Rafiq said, throwing his hands up in the air and backing away. "I didn't mean to . . . Aghhhh!"

"You son of a bitch!" Lavender said, stabbing him in the shoulder with the tip of a blue ballpoint pen. "Now get the fuck out. Leave your keys on the counter and go." Lavender slammed the door to the bar and headed up the back steps to her office. "And don't try no funny shit. I can see your every fuckin' move on camera," she said, turning around and hollering down the steps.

Rafiq pulled the pen out of his throbbing arm and threw it to the floor. A small, round open wound was the result of the ordeal. He then searched the liquor shelf for a bottle of vodka. He opened the bottle of Absolut and poured it down his arm to stop any infection that may have set in. Rafiq ripped one of the dishtowels in half and wrapped it around his arm. He huffed and puffed and slammed his fist on the surface of the bar.

"Fuck," he yelled out loud, kicking the stool behind the counter, causing it to fall over.

Rafiq was so pissed off that he was ready to kill Lavender. It would be nothing to him; he'd killed so many people while at war when he was in the army that he was immune to death. The thought automatically left his mind when he saw his wife's name flash across the screen on his cell phone.

"Hey, love," Rafiq said, smiling at the thought of her beautiful chocolate face.

"Hey, baby," Rafiq's wife sang into the phone. "What time are you coming home? I miss you."

"I'm locking up now," Rafiq said. "I need to talk to you about something when I get in."

"Oh my God! Did you get promoted to partner?" she squealed. "Lavender finally came to her senses, huh?"

Rafiq paused for a moment; there was no way he could tell his wife that he was just fired. "Yes, baby, I did. Your man is a partner, baby," he said, telling her exactly what she wanted to hear. "I'll see you when I get in."

"Okay, baby, I love you," she said. "Be careful on your way home."

"Okay, I will . . . I love you too, Farrah," Rafiq said, flipping his phone closed.

Rafiq turned off the lights to the club and left the keys on the bar as Lavender instructed. He knew that she couldn't run the place by herself. They had been through situations such as this in the past and she always wound up calling Rafiq back a day or two later. He was kind of skeptical because it never got as physical as it did this time around, but she would call—eventually. He was going to go home, tell his wife he was on vacation for the week, and enjoy his family.

Chapter 10

Monkey on My Back
Lavender

Lavender slammed the door to her office and went straight toward the security camera system, which was located behind her desk in a glass wall cabinet. She zoomed in on the camera affixed to the bar and watched as Rafiq grabbed the few belongings he had and headed toward the exit. Lavender grabbed her pistol from her office drawer and headed back downstairs to lock the door. She placed the safety in the off position and held it down to the side with her finger lying against the trigger. Once downstairs, Lavender made sure the bolt on the door was nice and secure. She knew she should have never promoted Rafiq in the first place. But the customers loved him and Lavender was all about keeping her customers happy. Once Rafiq turned thirty, he started losing his stamina in the bedroom and he was no longer eligible to be a working boy. So she figured she could use a little help with managing the place and decided to keep him on as a manager. She trusted Rafiq the most out of all of her employees; he was her first hire. She surveyed the bar and lounge area once more before trotting back upstairs to her office.

Lavender sat down at her desk, placed the safety back on her pistol, and slid it in the upper left drawer. She then pulled out the top right drawer, and removed a crystallized candy dish filled with cocaine. As she lifted it out, she noticed a picture stuck to the bottom of it. She pulled it away from the bottom of the dish and looked at it; it was a photo of her and her ex-fiancé, Ahmad, at a political event for his father. Tears welled up in Lavender's eyes as she thought about how happy she was with him. He made her life complete and promised that he would never hurt her.

He'd slept with her only sister and made plans to run away with her. Lavender's sorrow instantly became rage as she then thought of how foolish she was for trusting him. He stole her heart and for that, she took his life. She recalled Ahmad's facial expression as his last breaths wisped away; the horror in his eyes danced around in her mind as she took the top off of the dish and used her pinky nail to scoop out a small mound of coke. Ahmad had made Lavender hard; she vowed to never love again and she made good on her promise. Lavender closed her right nostril with her right index finger and held her pinky up to her nose. Lavender snorted the small mound of coke up like a vacuum cleaner and proceeded to scoop another. She closed her eyes and licked her lips as the high consumed her. All of a sudden, Lavender felt like she was on top of the world. She didn't need Rafiq to manage her club; she did it before without him and it would be nothing to do it again.

Beads of sweat trickled down the back of Lavender's neck as she rushed around the bar pouring drinks and placing them in front of the clients. She grabbed a dishtowel and patted at her forehead and threw it to the side. It had been a month since she fired Rafiq, and since then she hadn't had a single day off. She looked at the sink; it was overflowing with glasses and empty liquor bottles. The floor behind the bar was sticky from her spilling alcohol as she topped off drinks. Just as she was about to sit down and rest, Ming walked up to the bar and sat down.

"Hey, Ming, hon, what can I get ya?" Lavender asked, placing a coaster in front of her.

"A glass of chardonnay would be nice." Ming smiled, folding her hands in front of her at the bar. "But seeing Rafiq back in here would be even better."

"Excuse me? I didn't get the last of that . . . What did you say?" Lavender frowned, placing a wine goblet filled to the brim in front of her.

"Listen, love," Ming said, taking a sip from her glass. "We love you but things just aren't the same without Rafiq around. I mean look at this place," Ming said, peering over the bar at the sink and overflowing trash cans. "I'm starting to feel like I'm at a cheesy bar in the middle of Northern Liberties or something. I spend way too much money in here to have to be around this mess. The place is disgusting," Ming said, running her finger across the edge of the bar, which was also sticky. "If you don't do something soon I just might have to cancel my membership."

Lavender quickly surveyed the bar area. She was right; the place looked like a car wreck. All the ashtrays were full and the countertop surface was sticky. "Don't worry, Ming, I'll take care of everything. Please go have a seat over in the lounge area. I'll call you when it's time."

"I sure hope so, Lavender," Ming said, getting up from the barstool and grabbing her pocketbook from the seat beside her.

Lavender took a seat at the bar and buried her head in her hands. She closed her eyes, and all she could think about was getting a hit of cocaine.

"Hey, Lav," Keon said, sitting down beside her. "What's up with you?"

Lavender lifted her head up from her hands, took one look at Keon, and buried her head in her hands again. "Hey, K, you ready for your shift?"

"I've been here for two hours," Keon said, looking confused. "You okay? You look a little burned out."

"I'm a little tired is all," Lavender said, looking up again. "I haven't had a day off in weeks. My hair looks like shit, my nails are chipped. I really need a break," Lavender admitted.

"So what you gonna do?" Keon asked, rubbing her arm.

"I know what I'm not going to do," Lavender said, looking over at Keon. "I'm not calling Rafiq. I don't care how much Ming threatens to leave. He is a pain in the ass and I'm sick of his bullshit."

"Lav, what did you tell me when I first started here?" Keon asked, turning his head slightly to the side while looking in Lavender's slanted dark brown eyes.

"I don't know, I told you a lot of things," Lavender said, rolling her eyes.

Keon pointed his finger in the air and then said, "You told me that even though Rafiq was a jerk and an asshole, he always got the job done."

"And you telling me this because?" Lavender asked, crossing one leg over the other.

"I'm sayin' this to say that you are allowing your personal feelings for him to block your business sense. You can hate him all day, every day; the truth is, he gets the job done," Keon said, getting up from the bar. "I'ma leave you on that note. I got a client anyway. Ming over there getting impatient; she keep looking down at her watch and shit."

Lavender got up from the bar as well and returned behind the counter. She turned on the spigot and starting washing out glasses. Lavender couldn't fight the fact that Keon had a valid point. Lavender continued washing and drying the glasses and placing them in the racks; she dried off her hands and reached under the bar to grab her purse. She pulled out her BlackBerry and scrolled down until she came across Rafiq's number in her contact list. She pressed the talk button and placed the phone up to her ear.

"Yes," Rafiq sang into the phone. "To what do I owe the pleasure?"

Lavender sucked her teeth and then took a deep breath. "I want to talk to you. Can you meet me at the club tonight around eleven?"

"Sure, sure, we can talk," Rafiq said with a hint of cockiness in his voice. "I'll see you at eleven."

"A'ight then," Lavender said, "I'll see you then."

Lavender hung up the phone and stuffed it back in her purse. Part of Lavender already felt as though she had made a mistake by even calling Rafiq, but the other part of her was relieved. Lavender hadn't worked this hard in years. She poured herself a glass of bourbon and leaned against the bar. She kicked off her black open-toed Louboutin slingback heels and replaced them with a pair of red and white flip-flops from the dollar store. Lavender finished her drink and went to toss her glass in the sink. The stickiness from the floor caused her to stumble out of her right flip-flop and tumble to the floor. Lavender sat up and all she could do was laugh. She too felt like she was in a cheesy bar in the middle of nowhere. Lavender knew what she had to do: make Rafiq a sweet enough deal to get him back in the club without feeling like she was selling her soul to the devil. She got off the floor and headed straight to the janitorial closet to grab the mop and bucket.

Lavender checked the security camera before she let Rafiq in the club. She escorted him upstairs to her office and locked the door behind them. She looked across the desk at Rafiq. He was wearing a black waist-length leather motorcycle jacket with a maroon-colored Polo button-up. A heather gray Polo skully hat covered his head and a matching scarf hung loosely around his neck. A five o'clock shadow covered his face, as did a pair of gold Armani sunglasses.

"You look good," Lavender said, reaching over to hand him a Cuban and a cigar cutter.

"Thanks, you look . . . pretty good yourself," Rafiq said, cutting the tip of the cigar and placing it in the wastebasket beside the desk.

"Quit the bullshit, Rafiq. I know I look a mess," Lavender said, leaning over to light his cigar for him.

"You said it, I didn't," Rafiq said, throwing his hands up in the air. Rafiq took a few puffs from his cigar and then said, "So what's up? You said you wanted to talk. So here I am."

"I want you to come back and work for me," Lavender said, lighting a cigar and taking a puff.

"Lavender, I'm gonna be honest wit' you, I can't come back unless you make some changes around here," Rafiq said, continuing to puff on his cigar. "I feel like you never even think about considering anything that I propose when it comes to the club. I mean, I have some good ideas but you always shoot me down before you can even hear them." Rafiq leaned up from the seat and continued talking. "I put a lot of work in here and I feel like it goes unnoticed. I ain't had a raise in over a year and not once have you ever stopped to say thank you for my hard work."

Lavender felt as though she were talking to a bitch rather than a dude, but she kept her cool and played her part. "So what would you like to see happen around here?"

"First off, I want a raise. The cat's out of the bag, I know you know I was taking a few dollars here and there but I need a real raise. I got a family to feed. Secondly, I feel as though you should make me a partner. Come on, I been working for you for three damn years. I can run this place with my eyes closed."

"Okay, okay, here's my proposal," Lavender said, now leaning up from her seat and folding her hands in front of her on the desk. "I'm willing to give you an extra two hundred and fifty dollars a week in your check but no partner. I'm standing my ground on that one, you're just not ready, Rafiq. That's my final offer—take it or leave it."

Rafiq took a long drag on his cigar and blew the smoke in Lavender's face. "Five hundred dollars extra a week, take that or leave it. *And*, you have to be open to some of my ideas around here." Rafiq sat back in his chair and waited for Lavender's reply.

Lavender swatted at the smoke and then said, "Okay, okay, I can do that . . . So do we have a deal?" Lavender extended her hand for Rafiq to shake.

Rafiq reached over and shook her hand. "Yes, we have a deal."

"So I'll see you first thing in the A.M.?" Lavender asked, picking her cigar up from the ashtray.

"Yeah, I'll be here," Rafiq said, placing his cigar stump in the ashtray. "Oh yeah, one more thing."

"What is that?" Lavender asked, finishing off the remainder of his cigar.

"You might wanna get those little monkey nubs of yours manicured. I was starting to think you were part animal for a minute there." Rafiq wore a cunning grin on his face.

"Get the fuck outta my office," Lavender said, rolling her eyes. "See you in the morning." She chucked a set of keys at him and he caught them.

Rafiq nodded and headed toward the door.

Lavender propped her feet up on the desk and placed her hands behind her head. She was content with the outcome of their meeting and even happier to get back to her extracurricular activities. It had been some time since she had last fed her habit and she couldn't wait to satisfy her appetite. She opened the drawer and ran her hand across the top of the crystal candy dish where she kept her stash. She opened it up; and there were a few crumbs at the very bottom. She tried to use her pinky nail to scoop it out but it just wasn't enough. Lavender placed the lid back on the dish and closed the drawer. She grabbed her jacket and purse from the coat rack and flew down the steps. She dialed her cell phone as she locked up the club and got in her car.

"Hey, lady Lav, what can I do for ya?" a deep, raspy, Italian-accented voice answered.

"Hey, Al babe, I need the usual," Lavender said, starting the ignition to her car.

"I'm afraid I can't do that. The boss said you gotta pay your tab off before I can spot you again," Al said.

"Aww come on, Al," Lavender begged. "You know I'm good for it."

Al paused and then let out a loud sigh. "Okay, okay, but you gotta pay your tab by the end of the month; otherwise, the boss is gonna be real mad."

"Don't worry about it, I'll pay it next week—I promise," Lavender said, rocking back and forth, waiting for the car to warm.

"Okay, I'll have one of the boys deliver the package to you," Al said. "They'll be there in about a half hour."

"I'm on my way home now," Lavender said, pulling out of the parking lot. "Tell them to leave it with the night guard."

When Lavender arrived at her apartment building, it was close to 2:00 A.M. She stopped at the front desk and Willy, the night guard, was sitting on a stool, glued to his portable DVD player. She could hear moaning coming from the movie he was watching as she walked up to the front desk.

"Hello, Willy. How are you?" Lavender asked, clearing her throat in the process.

"Why hello there, Ms. Lavender," Willy said, pausing the movie and focusing all of his attention on her. "Another long night at the office?"

Lavender gave him a strange look and then it dawned on her that everyone in the building thought she was an entertainment attorney. There was no way they would have allowed her to move in the building without stating what she did to earn her money. They were very strict about what kind of residents they allowed to live in the building. Lavender had to fill out an application and go on two rounds of interview just to be put on the waiting list. It took her a year to get an apartment in the building and the only reason she got in was because one of the older tenants who lived there died.

"Yes, Willy, another long night I'm afraid," Lavender said, leaning on the desk.

"The courier left you a package," Willy said, reaching under the desk and returning with a medium-sized package wrapped in brown paper. "It seems like they get here later and later every time."

"Well, you know how it is, Willy, you may go home but the work never stops. I have some meetings to prepare for in the morning. Thanks for the package," Lavender said, signing it out on the log. "Have a good night, Willy."

"You too, Ms. Lavender," Willy said, tipping his hat, revealing his salt-and-pepper afro.

Lavender smiled as she placed the box under her arm and headed toward the elevators. She took one last look at Willy, who had come from around the desk to get a better look at her butt, and mumbled, "Dirty-ass old man."

Lavender opened the door to her apartment and traveled through it without turning on a single light until she reached her bedroom. She dumped the package on the bed along with her purse and headed toward the bathroom. She turned on the shower and stripped out of her clothes, leaving them on the floor. Lavender closed the shower curtain and closed her eyes and tilted her head back, allowing the warm water to splash down on her face. She snatched the Carol's Daughter Sugar-Dipped Vanilla shower gel and loofah from her shower caddy. Lavender lathered her entire body, leaving no crevice untouched. As she rinsed off, all she could think about was getting a taste of her new stash. Lavender pulled the curtain back and jumped out of the shower without so much as turning the water off. She made her way back to the bedroom dripping wet, leaving wet footprints across the cherry wood floor. She eyed the package as she sifted around her vanity table for her metal nail file. Still damp from the shower, Lavender crawled up on the bed and sat Indian style with the package in her lap and the nail file in hand. She peered down at the package and held the file up in the air, puncturing it with one swift movement. Cocaine poured out of the package and onto the bed. Lavender beamed as she scooped up a small amount with the tip of her nail file and held it to her nose. She closed her eyes, held her right nostril closed, and inhaled.

Chapter 11

Back in the Saddle
Rafiq

Rafiq held the door open to the club with his leg as he carried in two large boxes of supplies that were left out front by the UPS delivery man. He set them down at the door and ran back to his Range Rover to grab his cup of coffee and egg and cheese croissant. He pressed the alarm to his truck and disappeared in the club. Once inside, he turned on the flat-screen TVs in the lounge area and began prepping the bar for the day. He whistled as he restocked the liquor bottles and placed the glasses in the hanging rack above the bar.

It had been a month since he returned to the club and Rafiq hadn't had a single day off. There were some nights that he was at the club so late that he just decided to sleep over. His wife had been on his back for the past week about him not spending enough time with her or the family, but Rafiq figured she wouldn't mind once she found out that he had already put a down payment on the house they saw some time ago. She fell in love with it and although it was a bit pricey, Rafiq didn't care. She wanted what she wanted and it was his job as her husband to provide for her and their children. If everything went right, Rafiq would be able to purchase the house by the end of the month. Usually, he would have bitched and complained to Lavender about all the hours he was working but not this time.

When Lavender didn't show for work, he didn't even bother calling her; it was simply a waste of time anyway. She was so high that most of the time he didn't speak with her for days at a time. He didn't care; he loved being in charge of the club in her absence. In Rafiq's eyes, it ran better when she was out of the picture. They made more money and the clients were always satisfied.

Rafiq counted the safe as he did every morning before the club opened and noticed there was $5,000 missing. He recounted it two more times just to make sure he wasn't tripping. He closed the safe and dialed Lavender's number; when she answered he hung up. It was then that he remembered that he was no longer going to question her when money was missing. It was *her* club and, like she said, she could do whatever she downright pleased. He looked down at the stainless steel Movado watch his wife had just gotten him for his thirty-fifth birthday this past weekend; it was almost noon. Before he opened the doors for business, he went upstairs to check on the guys and make sure that they were ready to service clients.

He knocked on each door individually and looked them over, making sure they were well-groomed and presentable. When he arrived at Keon's room, he knocked but received no answer. He didn't recall seeing him this morning and it worried him. Rafiq looked at his watch once more and it was now noon. He hurried downstairs to open the door. There were three members waiting in the parking lot to get in. He held the door open and waited for all of them to pass before he locked it back up.

Rafiq took his rightful place behind the bar but he couldn't help to wonder where Keon was. It wasn't like him to be late or absent from work without calling. Rafiq skimmed the appointment book under his name; there was a 12:30 P.M. appointment with Ming crossed out with red pen. It was obvious that Lavender was back to her old tricks again. She loved to abuse her powers with the boys. She made them her personal smut puppies and Keon was no different. Rafiq slammed the book closed and shoved it back on the shelf. He knew that when Ming arrived and she found out her appointment had been canceled there would be hell to pay. He quickly texted her phone to let her know that Keon called out sick and hoped that she didn't piss a bitch. Rafiq's phone vibrated and there was a reply from Ming saying, "Cancel my membership." Rafiq shook his head; he couldn't wait to tell Lavender that Ming no longer wanted to be a member. Out of all of the members, Ming spent the most money in the club. With her canceling her membership, money was definitely going to be tight. There was no way that Lavender could say no to opening the doors to new clients now.

Rafiq searched the bar for the bottle of Wild Turkey Bourbon he hid a few days ago and poured himself a drink. Losing Ming meant that everyone was going to suffer. He continued to sip from his glass as he thought of ways that he could persuade Ming to change her mind. After a second glass, he realized that it was hopeless; Ming was too head strong to fall for any of Rafiq's tricks.

A loud knock echoed throughout the club; Rafiq already knew it was Lavender. She was the only person who refused to use the intercom system. Rafiq checked the camera that was situated at the front door and zoomed in; Lavender and Keon were standing there talking. Rafiq looked down at his watch again as he cruised over to the door to let them in; it was almost

1:00 P.M. He took the latch off the door and opened it wide enough for them to get in.

"Hey, hon," Lavender said, kissing Rafiq on the cheek as she passed him.

"You're looking refreshed," Rafiq said, looking her over. A yellow Balenciaga bag hung from her forearm and a pair of black Tom Ford sunglasses covered her eyes. Both the bag and the glasses were from the latest spring collections. Her signature china doll bob fell to her shoulders. M·A·C's Russian Red lipstick coated her lips and red nail polish covered her fingers and toes.

"Thank you." She smiled, revealing her sparkling white teeth.

"I have to talk to you about something," he said, looking at her then at Keon. "Keon, can you give us a minute?" Rafiq asked.

"Sure, sure, not a problem," Keon said, backing away and taking a seat on the opposite end of the bar.

"Did you cross Keon's appointment out with Ming this afternoon?" Rafiq asked, keeping his voice sweet and respectful. He really wanted to grab her and shake the shit out of her.

"Yeah, I did," Lavender said without hesitation.

"Well, Ming instructed me to cancel her membership," Rafiq said, folding his arms and leaning against the bar. "You know she's our best client."

Lavender frowned. "I'm gonna give her a call and see if I can persuade her otherwise." Lavender frantically searched through her cell phone until she came across Ming's number. She pressed the talk button and walked away.

Rafiq turned his attention back to Keon, who was sitting at the end of the bar with his earphones on, bobbing back and forth, silently lip-synching the words to Kanye West's "Good Life." Rafiq motioned for him to take off the headphones and come over to the middle of the bar where he was.

"You out moonlightin' wit' the boss, huh," Rafiq said, passing him two cans of Red Bull.

"Naw, it wasn't even like that," Keon said, taking a seat in front of Rafiq at the bar. He popped the top to one of the Red Bulls and took a sip. "We were handling some business."

"Being her personal fuck buddy is not handling business," Rafiq said, wiping the bar down with a damp dishrag. "It's the exact opposite. You know the club rules, man. Just because it's Lavender doesn't mean they don't apply."

"Come on, man, give me a break. I needed a couple of dollars and she propositioned me, so I handled my business," Keon whispered, looking over at the end of the bar to make sure Lavender wasn't listening. She was too engulfed in the conversation she was holding on her cell phone to even notice that she was the topic of discussion.

"So how much money did you sell your soul to the devil for?" Rafiq asked, grabbing the now empty can of Red Bull and chucking it in the trash can.

"Five grand," Keon said, opening the second can and taking it straight to the head.

"Oh really?" Rafiq said, putting two and two together. There was no doubt in his mind that the five grand that she paid Keon was from the safe. "Damn, man, at least get the game right if you gonna try and play it. You make more money from the clients. Why would you sell yourself so cheap for her? Because she your boss? You should have asked for at least a grand more than you get when you on the clock here at the club."

"I know, I know but my grandma been sick, man. I had to pay for her medication, it's crazy expensive.

Without it, she'll be dead. I can't lose her, she all I got, man," Keon said, leaning over the counter to toss the empty can in the trash.

Rafiq could definitely understand where he was coming from; he too had business to take care of. His family was the reason why he got up in the morning and he didn't know what he would do if anything happened to them. "A'ight, man," Rafiq said. "Just be careful hanging out with her. If the other guys peep you, it's gonna stir up a lot of trouble. Go get ready for your appointment."

"Who's it with?" Keon asked, getting up from the stool and grabbing his duffel bag from the floor.

"I believe you have Raji," Rafiq said, grabbing the appointment book from the shelf to make sure he was right. "Yeah, its Raji," he said, using his finger to confirm.

"Cool," Keon said heading toward the steps.

"She'll be here at two," Rafiq said, looking down at his watch once more. "You have a good twenty minutes to get yourself ready."

"That's more than enough time," Keon said, disappearing up the stairs.

Rafiq was really starting to dig Keon. He still had a strange feeling about him but he seemed like a pretty stand-up dude. What he liked most about Keon was that he was about his dough. He never fraternized with the other staff and he rarely had conversations with the clients. He did his job and went home. He just wished the other guys at the club were like him. His only concern was that he spent too much time with Lavender; usually when one of the guys got hooked up in her web they wound up strung out or turned out. Either way they wound up having to get rid of them. He couldn't lose Keon; he was the reason why business was booming. Rafiq vowed to keep a close eye on Keon and check him when he was slipping.

Rafiq edged toward the end of the bar where Lavender was, in hope of catching bits and pieces of her conversation with Ming. From the looks of Lavender's scrunched-up face, the conversation wasn't going so well. Rafiq knew that this would be the perfect time to talk to Lavender about taking on more members. Revenue would be down and that meant less money to support her habit. Rafiq turned his back to Lavender and acted as if he was dumping the ashtrays on the bar as she ended her conversation and tossed her cell phone on the bar.

She buried her head in her hands and then said, "Ming's out. I tried to convince her to stay. I even discussed giving her a credit to use at her leisure and she still insisted on canceling her membership."

"Well, maybe it's time to open the doors to some new members," Rafiq said, placing the ashtrays back on the bar and proceeding to fill up the napkin holders. "We haven't had new members in over a year."

"No, no, no," Lavender said, shaking her head from side to side. "No new members. I still think we'll be okay without Ming."

"Okay, if you say so," Rafiq said, trying not to press the issue.

"I'll be upstairs if you need me," Lavender said, pushing away from the bar.

Rafiq nodded and continued with his daily duties. He grabbed a cigar from the bar and headed outside for a quick smoke break. The sun poured down on his head as he stood outside the club and puffed on the cigar. The crisp spring breeze caused Rafiq's skin to prickle. He closed his eyes as he exhaled. When he opened them Keon was standing next to him in a pair of black pajama pants and a V-neck T-shirt.

"You done already?" Rafiq asked, looking over at Keon as he took another puff of the cigar.

"Yup, she up there trying to recuperate. I put a beating on that ass something vicious," Keon boasted, lighting a cigar.

"That's what's up," Rafiq said, giving him a pound. "With Ming gone, y'all gonna have to work extra hard to keep the money flowing around here."

"What you mean wit' Ming gone?" Keon repeated with a look of confusion forming on his face. "What happened?"

"You moonlightin' wit' ya girl is what happened," Rafiq said, leaning against the club door. "You had an appointment wit' her this afternoon and you missed it."

"Aww, man. I ain't know she was on the books for today . . . Damn, I'm salty as shit."

"It's not your fault," Rafiq said, finishing off what was left of his cigar. "Lavender's the one who crossed it out on the books."

"I'ma miss those tips," Keon said, continuing to puff on his cigar. "If I knew she was on the books, I woulda never said yes to Lavender last night. She just so damn aggressive, man. Lavender can be like a dude when it comes to sex. I was about to leave the club last night and she did everything in her power to make me go wit' her. Dawg, she fuckin' pulled my pants down to my ankles and begin sucking me off in the parking lot. There was nobody around but I'm sayin' . . . she still off the chain."

"Yeah, she is a hell cat when it comes to the bedroom," Rafiq said, grinning from ear to ear.

"Yo, you hit her too?" Keon asked, throwing the stump of his cigar down to the ground.

"Who hasn't hit her who works here?" Rafiq said, looking at Keon as if he were crazy. "There is no way she is going to hire a nigga she hasn't smashed before."

"So are y'all gonna replace Ming?" Keon asked, changing the subject back to the situation at hand. "'Cause y'all probably gonna have to get two or three people to make up for the money that she was spendin' up in here."

"Yeah, I've been trying to tell Lav that we need to recruit new members but she keeps insisting that we don't need any," Rafiq said, placing his hands in his jeans pockets. "I'm telling you, all we have to do is get five new members in here and we would be cool. Money would be fallin' from the sky out this muthafucka."

"Fallin' from the sky, huh," Keon repeated.

"Yup, fallin' from the sky, we all could be paid," Rafiq said, leaning up from the door. "You know what, K, since you and her all buddy-buddy these days you should holla at her about it." Rafiq opened the door to the club and held it for Keon.

"You know what, I just might do that," Keon said, stroking his facial hair as he reentered the club. "I got another appointment so I'll get at you lata," Keon said, walking past the bar and back upstairs to his room.

"A'ight, man, I'll see you later," Rafiq said, returning to the bar area. Rafiq amazed himself; Lavender may have said no to him but she was sure to say yes to Keon.

It was a little after one in the morning when Rafiq locked up the club. He couldn't wait to get home and climb under the covers with his wife. He pictured her in his arms as he pulled out of the parking lot and started his journey home. Farrah was Rafiq's high school sweetheart. She was just a freshman when they started dating; Rafiq was a senior. She got pregnant when she was fourteen with their eldest daughter and her mother wanted her to get an abortion. Rafiq begged her to keep the baby and promised that if she did, when he returned from the service, he would marry her. So on her eighteenth birthday, he took her to be his wife and never looked back. She was Rafiq's only true love—besides his children. Yes, he had sex with other women at the club and while he was away on active duty, but she held the key to his heart. Rafiq tried her cell phone as he motored up 95 South; it went straight to voice mail. He shrugged it off and continued on the highway until he reached his exit.

Rafiq noticed the lamp in the bedroom was off as he pulled into the driveway of their Bensalem home. It was unlike Farrah to turn the light off before he got home; she always waited until he was lying in the bed next to her to do so. He turned the car off and headed straight for the front door. Fife, their pet Pomeranian, charged him when he came through the door, biting at his pant leg in a playful manner. Rafiq picked him up and held him in his arms. He dropped his keys on the coffee table and continued upstairs. He petted his head and allowed Fife to lick him in the mouth as he went from room to room checking on all three of his children one by one. He bent over and sat Fife on the floor in the hallway as he approached the door to the master suite. He opened the bedroom door and kicked off his Gucci loafers. Fiddling with the button on his pants, Rafiq felt the wall for the light switch and flicked it on. He dropped his pants to the ground and pulled his Armani Exchange T-shirt over his head, revealing a well-toned chest and arms the size of a body builder.

Rafiq stood over his wife as she slept peacefully on her side of the bed; she wore a relaxed smile on her face. She looked like an angel from heaven; his angel. Rafiq's face grew fire engine red as he grabbed a fistful of her shoulder-length chocolate brown locks and flung her out the bed and onto the floor.

"Babe, what's wrong?" Farrah asked, looking up at Rafiq. Her naked body was sprawled across their cream-colored carpet.

"Who the fuck is that nigga?" Rafiq roared, pointing to his side of the bed. There lay a large, naked, muscular body, intertwined in their chocolate-colored bed sheets, fast asleep.

Farrah peered over the side of the bed from where she had fallen and a look of terror fell upon her. "Babe, I can explain . . ." She got up from the floor and grabbed Rafiq's forearm.

"Get out," he howled, smacking her across the ride side of her face, causing her to fall to the floor once more.

Farrah held the side of her face as she picked herself up from the floor. Her lip was busted and blood seeped from the corner of her mouth. She formed her lips to speak once more as she eased past him toward the bedroom door, but when she noticed the glazed-over look in his eyes she decided against it. She grabbed her robe from the back of her vanity chair and left as instructed.

Rafiq opened the doors to the walk-in closet located next to his wife's side of the bed and grabbed a metal lockbox from the very top shelf. He opened it up; inside lay the baby nine he bought his wife for protection some time ago. He took it from the container that had been its home and gripped it in his oversized left hand. He slid the safety off and exited the closet. Huge beads of sweat formed on his upper lip as he approached the side of the bed where the sleeping stranger lay. His heart raced as he approached his prey; he stood over him, silently studying his features. Rafiq couldn't understand how he could still be sleeping after all of what just went down with him and Farrah. Rage overtook his body as he thought about the good sex they probably shared to cause him to be in a deep sleep. There were plenty of nights when Farrah had put it on him so bad that it caused him to sleep like a log. Rafiq couldn't help to wonder what his wife saw in this man that would cause her to commit such an act. He placed his knee on the edge of the bed by the head of the stranger and pointed the gun at the side of his head. He eased back on the trigger. His eyes opened wide and before he could make a move, Rafiq delivered the shot to his temple.

Rafiq backed away from the bed like a zombie with the gun still in his hand and the safety still in the off position. He traveled down the hallway and found his wife huddled in the bed of his eldest daughter's bedroom with all three of the children surrounding her. He stood in the doorway with the gun down at his side and tears streaming down his face. He looked at his wife; the side of her face where he smacked her was swollen. She rocked back and forth with her knees pulled up to her chest as if she were a battered child being abused by her father.

"Get out of my house," Rafiq demanded, stepping into the room and pulling her away from the kids.

"I'm sorry, baby, please . . ." she pleaded, looking into his glazed-over eyes. "It was a mistake. I love you, Rafiq, please just listen to me for a second."

"I said get out," he repeated, lifting her up by her neck and throwing her against the wall outside the bedroom.

The kids screamed as her petite frame fell to the floor. Rafiq picked her up by the arm and ushered her down the hallway all while still carrying the gun in his hand. He pushed her down the steps and out the front door. He looked at his wife standing on the porch in her pink satin robe and barefoot; her hair was matted down on one side of her face from sweat and tears. Dried-up blood stained her lips and her eyes carried sorrow only she could bear; once his angel, she was now the devil's play toy. He slammed the front door in her face and placed the safety back on the gun. He then traveled to the kitchen and went straight for the refrigerator. He grabbed a cold beer and traveled back through the house to the living room. He plopped down in his favorite spot: a recliner his wife and the kids bought him for Christmas last year. He placed the gun on the side table beside him and chugged on his beer. Rafiq had a long night ahead of him; he had to go clean up. Draining the last drop out of the bottle, he placed it on the table beside the gun.

He wiped at his eyes and made his way back upstairs to rid himself of the stranger who ruined his marriage.

Chapter 12

Family Man
Keon

Keon hoisted Mariah on his shoulders started the short walk to the playground down the street from his house. Chevy walked beside him picking up leaves from the ground and tossing them on Keon in a playful manner. Keon lowered her to the ground as they reached their destination and held her hand until they reached the swing set.

Chevy sat on a nearby bench and watched as Keon continued to push Mariah on the swings. He seemd to be having more fun than she was; she never seen him smile so much in her life. What really put Chevy's heart at ease was the fact that Mariah finally had a father. Everything was working out just the way she wanted it and she couldn't have been happier. Chevy got up from the bench and walked over to Keon. She leaned against the gate behind the swing set with her hands folded and gave him a flirtatious smile.

Keon noticed there was something on her mind, she always smiled like that when she was about to ask him something important. "Spit it out," he said, pushing Mariah as hard as he could.

"So when are we going to move in together," Chevy said, out of nowhere. "We should be a family—you know . . . for Mariah and all."

"Move in together?" Keon asked, looking a little confused. "Don't you think it's a little soon for all that?"

"Just forget it," Chevy pouted, rolling her eyes. "You said you love me but you acting like you don't want to be with me and your daughter."

"No, I'm not acting like I don't wanna be wit y'all—it's just that with my job and all, it might not be a good idea." Keon said continuing to push Mariah on the swing.

"Why not?" Chevy said, leaning up from the gate. "You're a janitor not a secret agent."

Keon let out a loud sigh and then said, "I just don't think it's a good idea. Let's at least wait six months, that's all I'm askin. By then, my money should be right and I can leave the job I'm at to start my own business."

"Six months huh," Chevy said, sucking her teeth. "You promise."

"Scouts honor," Keon joked, throwing his hand up in the air as if he was a boy scout.

"Ok," Chevy said, shaking her head in agreement. "I can wait six months and not a moment later."

"Can we go now?" Keon asked lifting Mariah out of the swings and onto his shoulders. "It's getting dark outside and I know this little moneky right here is ready for dinner. He reached up and tickled her.

"Let's go," Chevy asked joining him by his side as they made their way back to his house.

Keon was awakened the next morning by loud banging on the door. Chevy jumped up from the bed and grabbed Mariah close. Keon slipped on his water shoes and headed downstairs in his pajama pants. A tall dark-skinned dude with a Sunni beard and bald head was peaking into the windows.

"Can I help you?" Keon asked opening the front door.

The stranger looked Keon up and down and then said, "Yeah, I'm lookin for Chevy. Her peoples told me I could find her here."

"Hold on for a second homie," Keon said, closing the door. He stood at the bottom of the steps and looked up at Chevy who looked as if she just seen a ghost.

"It's some dude at the door talkin about he looking for you," Keon said, looking at her sideways at this point.

Chevy took her time coming down the steps and she couldn't even look in Keon's face as she passed him to get to the front door. "Hey, Tim." Chevy stuttered. "What are you doing here?"

"I'm here to see my daughter. I been calling you for a fuckin month and you ain't been returning my calls. Your moms told me I could find you here." Tim said, looking over her shoulder at Keon whose arms were folded. "Who is the clown ass nigga behind you?" Tim asked, pointing at Keon.

"Clown?" Keon asked. "Don't get your feelings hurt out here nigga." Keon said sliding past Chevy and onto the porch where Tim was standing. "What you mean your daughter? Nigga that's my daughter."

Tim let out a loud laugh, "Oh yeah?" Tim said. "Well that's not what the birth certificate says."

Chevy looked back and forth at the two of them and she could tell by the looks on their face that things were about the get real ugly.

"Chevy, what the fuck is he talking about?" Keon asked, through gritted teeth. "I know you ain't fuckin tryin to play me."

"Yeah Chevy what he talking bout," Tim laughed, shaking his head at how silly Chevy looked. "Call me and let me know when I can pick up *my* daughter."

He said, looking over at Keon whose skin was turning bright red. He turned around and walked off.

Keon walked back in the house and took a seat on the bottom of the steps and folded his hands in his lap. His was trying not to snap out and give Chevy the chance to explain but his anger was getting the best of him. He took a few deep breaths and looked up at her. She was leaning against the closed front door which was located across from the stairs he was sitting on. Keon banged his fist against the wall in anger and then said, "What the fuck was that about?"

"K, I swear Mariah is your daughter—I would never lie to you about something like that." Chevy said, wiping the tears away from her face and onto her nightgown. "Its just that when you got locked up, Tim stepped up and took care of me and Mariah, He signed the birth certificate and everything. He has been acting as her father since she was born."

Keon held his head in his hands, "So why the fuck are you just telling me this now—huh?" he said, raising his voice. "You can't be trusted Chevy. I don't have time for these stupid young girl games you playin. You bringing niggas to where I rest my head at on some ole' bullshit and now you really want me to believe that Mariah's my kid?"

"Tim knows he's not her real father. Please don't be like this. I need you—I mean Mariah needs you," Chevy sobbed.

"This is what we gonna do," Keon said, lifting his head from his hands and looking at Chevy. "We're gonna get a paternity test and if Mariah's mine, I'm going to handle my business. As far as you and me are concerned," he said, pointing at her and then at himself. "We're done . . . I don't want nothin' to do wit you. You still playin' these childish ass games. When we met back up I thought that you had your shit together but now I see that you're the same silly bitch you were when we were fuckin' wit each other back then. As much as I love you Chevy, I'm not gonna let you and any other bitch get me in a situation that's gonna get me put back in the pen. So pack your shit up and I'm gonna call you and Mariah a cab to take you back to your mom's crib."

"Please, don't do this," Chevy cried. "We were supposed to move together . . . you promised."

"Get out of my face with that bullshit Chevy," Keon, said getting up from the steps. He walked over to the kitchen to use the phone so he could call a cab.

Chevy stomped up the steps and gathered the few things of hers and the baby's that she had at his house. She stuffed them in two shopping bags and kicked them down the steps; they landed by the front door. She then awakened the baby and put her coat on her over her pajamas. Chevy couldn't help to think about how much of a grave mistake she made by not telling Keon about Tim. The thought of Keon leaving her again made her want to kill herself. She hated Tim but she needed someone to help her with the baby. It wasn't her fault that Keon got locked up; he left her first. She grabbed her daughter from the bed and carried her on her hip. By the time she got downstairs, the cab was waiting in front of the door.

"Are you sure you want to do this," she asked, standing on the porch with the baby in her arms.

"Chevy don't talk to me like I'm making a mistake. You can't be trusted. Let's just get the paternity test done and take it from there. Regardless of the outcome, you and me will never be." Keon said, grabbing the two bags from the doorway. He walked her and the baby to the car and held the door as she got in. He then handed her the two bags she packed and closed the door.

"It's your loss," Chevy yelled loud enough for him to hear through the window and ordered the driver to pull off.

Keon shook his head and made his way back in the house. He closed the front door and turned around to go back upstairs to bed. He was startled when he noticed his grandmother was standing right behind him. "Hey Big Mom," he said, giving off a fake smile. He kissed her on the check and tried to ease past her in hopes of getting out of the long lecture he knew that was coming. He could tell from the scowled look on her face, that she wasn't happy with the events that had just taken place. He was hoping that she slept through all of the commotion but he ought have known better. Keon grabbed the banister and started up the steps.

"Come on and sit at the table and have a cup of tea with your Big Mom," She said, using her cane to maneuver through the living room. Once she reached the kitchen, she turned on the kettle and took a seat.

Keon rolled his eyes and came back down the steps. He followed her in the kitchen and took a seat across from her at the table.

"So what was all that commotion going on down here this morning?" He grandmother asked.

"Me and Chevy just had a few words Big Mom, that's all," Keon said, trying to keep it simple.

"Must have not been just a few words. The child done up and left Keon. Now, you know Big Mom don't like to pry but when I'm awaken out of my sleep in the middle of me dreaming about Luther Vandros, then we got a problem. Why did she leave son?"

"Some nigga came here asking for her and the baby," Keon said, rubbing his head with his hand. "He said that Mariah was his daughter."

"Aww baby, I'm sorry to hear that," Big Mom said, grabbing his hand from across the table. "I know that little girl meant everything to you."

"Yeah, she did," Keon admitted. "We're going to get a paternity test done. I'm hopin' she is mines Big Mom. I love that little girl."

"Don't worry about it, everything will work out fine," his grandmother said, pulling away from him to get the kettle. "Put it in God's hands son, and everything will be fine."

"I know Big Mom, I know. I just can't help it though. I trusted her and she straight played me," Keon said trying not to get overly emotional. He wiped at his eyes which were a little watery. "I'm gonna talk to her about getting the test done next week. I need to know if she is mines and I need to know as soon as possible."

"So what about you and that girl?" Big Mom asked, pouring hot water from the kettle into the tea cups.

"Me and Chevy? Nah, I can't be with her Big Mom. I love her, but I love me more. She's not worried about me having a relationship with Mariah. She's worried about me and her. If she lied about this she will lie about anything. She just can't be trusted." Keon said, grabbing the tea cup from his grandmother's hand and taking a sip. "Now, I gotta watch my back cause that dude know where I stay. I don't need no beef with no nigga over a chick."

His grandmother returned to the table with a cup of tea for herself and sat down. She could see the hurt in her grandson's eyes and it didn't sit right with her soul. She knew about the baby but she never once mentioned it to Keon. She felt as though it wasn't her place to get involved. Plus, she had heard from several people in the neighborhood that Chevy was promiscuous. She'd come to the house several times while Keon was locked up asking for money for pampers and formula. She knew Chevy never used it for the child because the little girl always looked raggedy.

"Everything will be fine. Don't worry baby," Big Mom assured him. "Everything will be just fine." She reached over and grabbed his hand. In the back of her mind, she was trying to convince herself of the same thing.

Chapter 13

Where's My Money
Lavender

"Hello," Lavender sung into the phone as she pulled into the parking lot at the club.

"You got my money?" a deep, raspy voice asked.

"Hello? Who is this?" Lavender asked, turning off the car and grabbing her cream-colored Gucci satchel from the passenger's seat.

"Stop playin' wit' me, bitch, you know who this is. If you don't have my money at the end of the week, I'ma blow your fuckin' head off."

"I . . . I . . . I just paid Al five thousand last week," Lavender stuttered, checking to make sure all of her car doors were still locked. She rolled the windows up as well paying special attention to her rearview mirror. Lavender didn't see anyone; she felt somewhat relieved.

"I don't give a fuck about no measly five grand. I want all my money. Bitch, you owe me forty-five."

"Forty-five grand? No, I paid Al five so I should only owe thirty-five now," Lavender said, correcting him on his error.

He laughed into the phone. "You silly bitch. Did you think you was gonna owe me my money for over three months now and not get taxed? Like I said, you owe me forty-five grand. If my money ain't sittin' in my hands by 9:00 A.M. on Friday morning, I'm gonna have your head blown the fuck off." The phone instantly disconnected.

Lavender dialed Rafiq's cell as fast as her thumbs would allow; her heart felt as though it was going to jump out of her chest as she waited impatiently for him to answer.

"Hey, Lav, what's up?" Rafiq said, hollering over the loud televisions playing in the background.

"What took you so long to answer the phone?" Lavender asked, surveying her surroundings. "I'm in the parking lot. Come and meet me at my car."

"Why?" Rafiq asked, walking over to a client and handing her the change for her drink.

"Damn, what's with all the questions? Just do it," Lavender replied and hung up.

Lavender watched as the door to the club opened and Rafiq came strolling out. She jumped out of the car and rushed over to meet him.

"What the hell is wrong with you?" Rafiq asked, stopping in the middle of the parking lot.

"Nothing," Lavender said, looking over her shoulder as she walked alongside Rafiq to the front door. Once inside, Lavender swung open the door to the bar and dropped her bag on the floor. She bent down and pressed in the code to the safe and started counting; there was only twenty grand available.

"Where's the rest of the money?" she asked, counting it again for a second time.

"It's all there," Rafiq said, standing over her. "I paid the boys for the week, all the bills for the month, and that's all that's left." Rafiq handed her the finance log.

Lavender grabbed it from him and skimmed through it; everything seemed to add up as he said. "Fuck!" Lavender yelled. "It's not enough!"

"It's not enough for what?" Rafiq asked, stepping out of her way as she stood up from the floor.

"Never mind," Lavender said, rushing past him and up the steps to her office.

She stood in front of the door and fiddled with her keys. Her hand was so shaky that she was having trouble opening it up. Once inside, Lavender crawled under her desk and punched in the code to the safe she kept mounted under it. She opened it up and pulled out two big stacks of money with rubber bands around them. She sat with her legs crossed as she counted each stack; it was thirty grand—even. Lavender sat there with the money sprawled across her lap and racked her brain as she thought about who she could get to loan her the rest of the money. Lavender couldn't use all the money in the safe; she would be flat broke and unable to keep the club open. To Lavender, keeping the club open and functioning properly was more important than paying off her debt. She needed at least ten grand on hand to continue to keep the club running smoothly. She couldn't ask Rafiq; she didn't need him in her business. Lavender cursed herself for being such a fool and getting herself into this type of trouble. She promised herself that if she got out of this situation she would never do coke again. She would go to rehab or do whatever she needed to stay clean. As she rubber banded the money and placed it back in the safe, there was a faint knock at the door.

"Who is it?" Lavender asked, scrambling to get up from the floor.

"It's K," Keon replied, turning the knob on the door.

"Come in," Lavender said, sliding into her office chair and crossing her legs as if everything was cool. In the back of her mind, all she could think about was getting her head blown off if she didn't come up with that moncy by the end of the week. It was already Wednesday afternoon; it was almost impossible to think where she would get ten grand on such short notice.

"What's up, Lav, we still on for tonight?" Keon asked, sitting on the edge of her desk.

"Sorry, hon, I think I'm gonna have to cancel," Lavender said, staring into space.

"What's wrong?" Keon asked, getting up from the desk and taking a seat in one of the two chairs that sat in front of her massive oak desk.

"I'm having some financial issues right now," Lavender blurted out without thinking.

"Everything cool? The club ain't in trouble, is it?" Keon asked, leaning up from the chair. He folded his hands in his lap and waited worriedly for a response.

"I'm afraid it might be," she said, tearing up. "I owe someone some big money and I'm short." Lavender didn't know why she was sharing this information with Keon, but there was something about him that made her feel safe. He reminded her of her ex-fiancé in so many ways—minus the cockiness.

"How much you owe?"

"Forty-five grand," Lavender said, grabbing a tissue from the box on her desk to wipe her eyes. "I'm short ten grand. I don't know what I'm going to do."

"Listen, I have a couple dollars stacked up." Keon hesitated. "I can loan you the money but you gotta stop snortin' that shit—fo' real."

Lavender shot Keon a dirty look. "What are you talking about?"

"Don't act stupid, Lav, everybody in here know you got that monkey on your back. All I'm sayin' is that I don't have a problem loaning you the money but I need it back."

Lavender looked like a little kid who had just gotten caught with her hand in the cookie jar. "I just started doing it a few months ago . . . I'm going to stop . . . I swear."

"I'ma help you out this time but if I find out you still doing that shit, I swear, man, it's a wrap. I'm not gonna have anything to do with you anymore in or outside the club."

"I'm telling you, I'm done with it," Lavender said, opening up her desk drawer and removing the crystallized candy dish where she kept her stash. She lifted it up so Keon could see it and tossed it in the trash can, shattering it into large pieces. "I can't believe you really lookin' out for me like this, K—that's why I like your ass so much. You're a real good dude."

"I'm not doing it for you, per se," Keon said, giving off a stern look. "I'm doing it for the club. I need this place as much as you do right now. I need my money to keep flowing like it has been for the past six months."

"So can you have the money for me by tonight?" Lavender asked, tilting back in her seat.

"Yeah, come by my place and get it," he said, getting up from the chair.

"I'll be there," Lavender said, getting up from her seat as well. She walked over to the door alongside Keon and held it open for him to exit.

"You know what else you need to do?" Keon asked, stopping in the doorway.

"What?"

"You need to get a few new clients up in here. Ever since Ming left it's been dry. A nigga practically gotta hang from the fuckin' ceiling to get a decent-ass tip these days."

Lavender chuckled. "Oh yeah? Well I tell you one thing, you don't have to hang from the ceiling for me."

She tugged at his pants and bit her lip. "We can still get it in like we planned tonight."

"And how are you going to pay me?" Keon said, reminding her of her financial situation. "I should be asking you what type of tricks you gonna turn for me out this camp." Keon grabbed at his crotch and licked his lips; his manhood grew as he looked Lavender up and down. Her wife beater clung to her chest like a baby sucking on a nipple. Her denim miniskirt barely covered her panty line.

With that being said, Lavender grabbed his arm, pulled him back in the office, and shut the door. She wrapped her arms around his neck and bit her bottom lip. "So what tricks you want me to turn, Special K?"

Keon grabbed at his crotch; his dick was so hard that it felt like it was going to explode. "Get on them knees and show me how special I really am," Keon said, grabbing her forcefully by the back of her neck and pressing his lips against hers. He then pushed her down between his thighs and loosened his pants, pulling his hardened member out in the process. He took the tip of his dick and rubbed it against her lips. He then squeezed her jaw as a signal for her to open her mouth. He stuffed his stiff shaft between her parted lips, causing it to hit her tonsils. She gagged as he pushed her head close to his body and guided himself in and out of her.

Lavender pushed his hand away and started going to town, slurping on him as if he were a melting Popsicle on a ninety-degree summer day. She gathered a gob of saliva in her mouth, spit it on his dick, and begin working her hand up and down his shaft like a madwoman. She continued to kiss, lick, and suck on his dick while stroking it with her right hand and massaging his sack in her other. She stuffed the tip of his dick back into her mouth until it reached her tonsils and she started to gag again.

"Oh shit," Keon howled, steadying himself against the door. "I'm about to cum. Damn girl," Keon said, holding her head close to his pubic hair as he released his hot liquids into her mouth.

Lavender pushed away from his body and opened her mouth, allowing his hot liquid to run down her lips and onto her chin. "How was that?" she asked, getting up from her knees and grabbing a tissue from her desk to catch her spillings.

"Right on time," Keon panted, fastening his pants. "So um, what you gonna do about getting some new clients up in here?" Keon asked, returning to the subject at hand.

Lavender sighed and then said, "I'll have Rafiq handle it. I'ma gonna try to have some new members in here by the end of the month."

"Don't try." Keon smirked, opening the door to the office. "Do."

"Yeah, yeah, yeah. I got you," Lavender said, sitting on her desk with her legs wide open, revealing a G-string the size of the slit of her pussy.

"Oh, by the way," Keon said, staring at Lavender like a dog in heat, "you still got a little cum on the side of ya mouth . . . Handle that," he said, opening the door and strolling out like he ran the place.

Lavender quickly turned to the side and wiped her face with the back of her hand; she laughed inside at how cocky Keon was. She had to admit, hiring Keon was one of the best things that ever happened to the club. What she really liked about him was the fact that he was honest and for the most part he stayed to himself. He gave sound advice and never acted on emotion. He was everything Rafiq wasn't and would make a perfect partner. Sure, Rafiq knew his job; he could do the paperwork, balance the books, and make a hell of a drink. His problem was that he based his decisions on who he liked rather than what was good for the business. Lavender jumped down from the desk and followed Keon down the hall.

"Special K, wait up," she said, picking her pace up to join him.

"What's up?" Keon asked, grabbing the doorknob to his room.

Lavender motioned for him to go in and she followed him and shut the door. She stood with her arms folded against her chest and smiled. "Why don't you be my partner. That way you can consider the money you gave me as an investment and I cut you in."

"Partner?" Keon repeated, taking a seat at the top of the king-sized bed and folding his hands in front of him. "I don't know nothing about running no business."

"Didn't you say you wanted to open your own cleaning business? Well this will be the perfect way to learn how to run one," Lavender said, taking a seat next to him.

"How so? I mean *this* and a cleaning business are two different things."

"Not really," Lavender said, glancing over in his direction. She got up from the bed and stood in front of him. "Listen, you can learn the foundation here, the bookkeeping, managing payroll, supplies, and of course customer service. You already good at customer service." A huge grin slid across her face. "Come on, just give it a try. I mean why not? You can start with coordinating the recruitment of new members with Rafiq."

"You really think I can pull this off? Or you just tryin' to make me partner so you don't have to give me my money back?"

"I think you're made for this. I mean, you have good qualities. You came in here and turned this place around so why not? *Plus* you'll get an extra five grand a month just because you're a partner."

"Okay, okay, I'll try it out," Keon said, leaning on his forearms.

Lavender got up from the bed and extended her hand in his direction. If she didn't know anything else, she knew the whole money thing would get him. "Partners?"

Keon leaned up from the bed and shook her hand. "Partners."

"A'ight, well, I'll see you later on to pick up that cash," Lavender said, heading toward the door.

Lavender still had reservations about taking on new members; it was always a risk. Member recruitment was always done by referral from current members but that meant more people knew about her operation. More people meant more of a chance that she would get pinched. Lavender liked to fly under the radar; if that meant losing a couple dollars to keep her club safe then so be it. But Keon was right, things were starting to get slow so she had no choice. She'd only recruited members twice in the club's lifetime, and both times she'd had to weed a few out. They either lied on their applications about their financial earnings, and when the income verification came back they got found out, or they wound up falling for the employees, which caused them to be put out.

As Lavender made her way back down the hall toward her office, she couldn't help but think about how far she had come since the club opened. She had her snags in her life but she made it through. She had lofty goals, and her drug habit was causing her to lose sight of them. Lavender had dreams of moving to Atlanta and opening a club up there. She looked at some real estate awhile back and even saved up enough to put a nice down payment on a building, but she wound up hitting her stash here and there to support her habit and when she looked up it was gone. There was no way in the world she was going to allow herself to owe anyone this type of money again in life.

Lavender dialed Al's cell phone as she approached the office door and waited for him to answer.

"I got the money," Lavender blurted out before he could say so much as hello.

"Good, good," Al said, coughing into the phone. "When can I pick it up?"

"Tonight, I'll leave it with the night guard at my building," Lavender said, taking a seat at her desk.

"So I guess you wanna place an order too, huh," Al said, continuing to cough in between his words. "How much you want?"

"Nope, I'm done wit' that shit," Lavender said proudly. "Just have your guy pick up the money and you'll never have to worry about me again."

"You sure about that, hon?" Al asked with a hint of sarcasm in his voice.

"Never been surer in my life."

Chapter 14

Stackin' Paper
Keon

"So how you been, man?" Keon asked, sitting across from Marquise, who was dressed in a gray shirt with matching gray pants.

"As good as can be expected, man," Marquise said, leaning back in his seat and folding his hands in front of him on the metal table. "What's been up wit' you? I see you lookin' good over there wit' ya fresh Polo boy on." Marquise peeped under the table and took a look at Keon's footwear. "Damn, homie, you got them new Air Maxes on, too, huh."

"I'm doin' a'ight, man," Keon said, folding his hands across his chest. "I'm just workin' hard, ya know, trying to stack some change—that's all."

Marquise chuckled and a sly smirk spread across his face. "Working hard, huh? Nigga, who you think you foolin'? I know what you out there doin'. You keep fuckin' wit' that broad Lavender if you want. Word on the street is that bitch got a serious coke habit and she owe some niggas some serious change."

"Well as long as she got my money right I don't give a fuck what she do or who she owe," Keon said, looking over at the clock on the wall. "Listen, man, I gotta go. I put some money on your books, you should be cool for a few months." Keon backed up from the table and stood up from his chair.

"Wait, man," Marquise said, looking up at Keon. "I'm not tryin' to hate on you, seriously. Just be careful wit' that broad. Be careful at that club . . . period. Don't be so fuckin' hardheaded all the time. Stack your paper and get out."

Keon looked at Marquise as if he were one of those special kids who rode on the short yellow bus. "Me hardheaded? Why don't you take your own advice for a change? If you wasn't so damn hardheaded you wouldn't be in this situation right now. I'm gonna tell you like I told you before—I got this."

"A'ight, man, you got it," Marquise said, throwing his hands up. "I just don't wanna see nothing bad happen to you out there."

"Man, I don't wanna see nothing bad happen to *you* in here," Keon said, nodding at the guard across the room to let him know that he was ready to leave. "I'll see you next month."

"Yeah, a'ight, man," Marquise said, standing up so the guard could place the cuffs on his wrists.

Keon walked away from the table without looking back. Once outside the detention center, Keon called a cab and waited patiently for it to arrive. His mind raced as he thought about Marquise; he wasn't concerned about Keon before. He was sick of him trying to act as if he really cared now. Marquise was just jealous; Keon was finally winning and on his way on top. He'd made partner, and only in a matter of months. Yeah, it cost him a few dollars, and that set him back with starting his own business, but in his mind it was an offer that he just couldn't refuse. When the cab arrived, Keon instructed the driver to take him straight to the club. He pulled his iPod out of his pocket and zoned out to prepare for the long night ahead of him.

By the time Keon arrived at the club it was a little past 5:00 P.M. He stood in the parking lot, waiting for the door to open. The sun beamed down on his reddish brown hair, causing sweat to pour from his forehead. He wiped the sweat away with the inside of his wrist and rang the bell again. Just as his patience was wearing thin, Rafiq's eyes peeked out of a small opening in the door.

"What's up, man," Keon said, grabbing the door and opening it wide. He shook Rafiq's hand and took a seat at the bar. He dropped his duffel bag beside him and waited for Rafiq to return to the other side of the bar so he could pour him a drink. Keon looked at Rafiq; for some reason, he didn't look like his old self. His eyes were red and he hadn't had a haircut in over a month.

"Nothin' much, man," Rafiq said, avoiding eye contact. "Just trying to take it easy—that's all."

"Come on, man, I ain't known you that long but I know something's up wit' you."

"Just going through some shit at home, that's all," Rafiq confessed.

"I know this might seem corny, man, but if you wanna talk about it, I'm here."

"Yeah, you was right," Rafiq said, glancing over at him as he washed out some glasses and placed them in the drain.

"Right about what?"

"That shit sounding corny," Rafiq said, continuing to wash out glasses.

"Whateva, man," Keon said, flagging Rafiq. "I was just trying to be a friend, man, that's all."

"Friend—huh," Rafiq said, dunking more glasses into the soapy water and washing them out. "Let's be honest. I know you don't like me, K, so why act like you do now?"

"Naw. I do think you can be a dickhead at times, but I don't have no problem wit' you. You just seem like you had a lot of shit on your mind. Plus, look at you. You look like shit—your hair ain't cut, your clothes are wrinkled. I ain't never seen you look like this before."

"Yeah, if you found your wife in the bed with another man you would look like this too," Rafiq mumbled, hanging the glasses in the rack above the bar.

"Aww, man, I'm sorry to hear that shit." Keon said, "I understand why you ain't want to talk about it in the first place."

"I can't believe she did that shit to me," Rafiq said, shaking his head in disgust. "I gave her everything . . . everything. She never wanted or needed for anything . . . Ungrateful bitch."

Keon didn't know whether to say anything or to remain quiet. From the look of Rafiq's face, he looked as if he could snap at any minute. "Don't worry, man, it'll be okay. You deserve better. There's someone else out there for you, dawg."

"Someone else?" Rafiq was taken aback. "And give her the satisfaction of divorce. Hell naw, I ain't going nowhere and neither is she. She gonna have to deal with me for the rest of her days. I already told her if she even so much as think about getting a divorce I was going to blow her fuckin' brains out."

"Damn, man, for real? I know you fucked the bull up, right?"

Rafiq looked over at Keon and shook his head. "Humph," Rafiq said, finishing up with the glasses. "Fuckin' him up is an understatement—I cold rocked that nigga. Ain't no man gonna come up in my house and have sex with my wife and think he gonna get away with it."

"Damn, man, that shit crazy," Keon said, reaching over the bar and grabbing a cigar out of the box. He cut the tip off and lit it. There was something about Rafiq that always gave him the impression that he was a closet crazy dude, but Keon always tried to give everybody the benefit of the doubt. If he learned anything in jail, it was don't judge a book by its cover.

"What you drinkin' on?" Rafiq asked, changing the subject.

"I don't know, surprise a nigga," Keon said, taking short puffs from his Cuban. "I got a long night ahead of me."

Rafiq turned his back and begin mixing up several top shelf liquors and topping it off with a splash of Red Bull. He placed a coaster in front of Keon and put the glass on top of it. "So did you get a chance to talk to Lavender about taking on more clients?"

"Yeah, man, I talked to her about it yesterday," Keon said, taking a sip of his drink.

"So what she say, man?" Rafiq asked, looking over at Keon while continuing to wipe down the bar.

"She game, as a matter of fact. She said you and I could do the recruitment." Keon said, taking a puff from his cigar.

"You and I?" Rafiq was taken aback. "Why would she say that? I don't need any help doing recruitment."

"Well, she suggested that I help out now that me and her partners and all."

"Partners?" Rafiq said, stopping in mid wipe and throwing the dishrag in the sink. "How did that happen?"

"She asked me yesterday when I talk to her about taking on new members. I didn't want to do it at first but she insisted." Keon finished his drink off and pushed the glass to the side. "A'ight, man, I gotta go get ready for work. I'ma holla at you lata about setting up the interviews for the new members."

"Cool," Rafiq said, forcing a smile across his face. "I'm going to go holla at Lavender right quick. I'll see you lata."

Keon threw his duffel bag back on his shoulder and headed toward the steps. He could tell by the redness of Rafiq's face that he wasn't happy about him becoming partner. Keon wasn't concerned though; he wasn't there to step on Rafiq's toes. All he wanted to do was make sure that his investment was protected and that business was booming enough to make his money back. Besides, truth be told, he was tired of sleeping with several women every night. He knew niggas would kill to be in his position but it was starting to drain him. By the time he got home at night all he wanted to do was sleep, and on his days off he was so busy helping his grandmother out around the house that he barely had time to himself. All he wanted to do was make his money back and open his janitorial business. According to his calculations, if they added a few new faces to the club, he could make his dough back in no time. Keon planned on working at the club for another six months to save a few more dollars and that was it. He wasn't going to be like the rest of the dudes there; they were caught up in the money. The good thing about it was, now that he was a partner he would always make profit from the club, and that suited him just fine.

Keon took one last look in the mirror and straightened his tie. The gray Armani suit he was wearing was perfectly tailored to his muscular frame. His black Prada lace-ups were so shiny that he could see the reflection of his face in them. Keon felt so uncomfortable in the suit that it was taking him forever to get ready. He was already running twenty minutes behind schedule. All the other guys were on the floor mingling and entertaining the guests. Tonight was the open house for the potential new members and there was a full house downstairs. He sprayed a mist of Issey Miyake in front of him and stepped in to ensure that his scent wasn't overpowering, and headed toward the door. Once downstairs, he began working the crowd, conversing with old members and greeting their guests, who were potential members. As Keon made his way through the crowd, and toward the bar, he bumped into a short Spanish woman, causing her to spill her drink on her dress.

"I'm so sorry, miss," Keon said, grabbing a handful of napkins from the bar to treat the stain on her shirt, without so much as really looking at her. He handed them to her and watched as she dabbed at the red splotch that covered her cream-colored minidress.

"Don't worry about it, love. I'm pretty sure the dry cleaner should be able to get it out. By the way, I'm Toni," she said, extending her hand to shake his.

Keon looked up and was met by the most beautiful green eyes he'd ever seen in his life. "Special K," he said, taking her hand and kissing it. "Nice to meet you as well. Let me get you another drink. What was that you were drinking in the first place?"

"Merlot," she responded, snatching her hand back in a shy manner. She blushed from ear to ear as Keon left and returned from the bar with a glass in hand.

"So are you enjoying yourself thus far?" he asked, placing the glass in her hand.

"Yes, very much so," she said, taking a sip from the glass. "There are some very handsome men here. I can understand why Susan loves it here."

"Oh, Susan's your sponsor?" Keon asked, continuing to drink in her features. Her hourglass shape reminded him of that of J. Lo. Her full-pout lips were painted a soft pink, as were her eyelids. Her hair was swept up in a soft bun.

"Yes, Susan is my sponsor. She and I are colleagues," Toni said, sipping from her drink.

"That's nice. Yeah, Susan is real good peoples," Keon said. "So, Toni, what do you do when you're not working?"

"I work out a lot . . . I'm sort of a gym rat. I love doing outside activities. During the summer I play touch football and I'm also on a rowing team."

"Wow, you're a busy woman," Keon replied, looking at her well-toned body. Her arms reminded him of Tina Turner's.

"Well, I have to keep fit, you know. No man wants an overweight woman."

"I hear you," Keon said, looking around the room. He caught Lavender's gaze; it was clear that he was taking up too much time with this one person. "Well it was nice to meet you, Toni. I look forward to seeing you again," he said, grabbing her hand and kissing it once more.

"Nice to meet you, Special K," Toni said. "I hope to see you again as well."

Keon nodded good-bye and continued to mingle with the crowd. He stopped here and there, and laughed and joked with the clients as well as his fellow employees until it was just about midnight. He collapsed on a stool at the corner of the bar and loosened his tie. From the looks of the meet and greet, there were a lot of good prospects. He enjoyed meeting all of the potential members, but he couldn't help but keep thinking about the one woman, Toni. Her beauty was so raw and natural that he could tell that, even without the makeup, she was just drop-dead gorgeous. He couldn't understand why a woman like her would want to participate in an operation such as this. Yes, there were pretty women who were members at the club, but they were all middle-aged women who were divorced, had children, grandchildren, or were just so tired of dating that all they wanted was to be dicked down good every once in a while. This woman looked all of about maybe thirty years old, and from her curves and flat stomach, she looked as if she had no kids at all. It was clear that she could find a man if she wanted, and fast.

Keon placed his head in his hands and closed his eyes; he needed a break. What he would do for someone to rub his feet and back for him like he did for so many others. No one ever asked him how his day was and what was on his mind. He just went in, did his job, and that was it; most of the time they were gone when he returned from the bathroom. They left him tips on the nightstand and that was it, not even a simple goodbye. He couldn't believe he was starting to feel this way. Eight months ago, when he first started the club, it never bothered him. Now he hated it. Keon wanted out sooner rather than later. He didn't know how much more he could take. Now he understood why a lot of people in this line of work used drugs. It was the only way they could cope with such a cold, heartless lifestyle for such a long period of time. For Keon, drugs were not an option; he'd quit before he allowed himself to go that far. The only thing he wanted to be addicted to was his freedom, and in four months his parole would be over and he would no longer have to worry about it being taken away. Keon forced himself up from the bar and headed to his room. He was going home to the only woman he knew would love him no matter what: his grandmother.

Chapter 15

Backstabber
Rafiq

Rafiq paced back and forth in front of Lavender's office door. His fists were clenched at his sides and his face was redder than a ripe tomato. He pounded on the door and then entered without waiting for her to ask who it was, startling Lavender, who was talking on her cell phone.

"How the fuck you just gonna make him partner—just like that?" he asked, leaning over the desk and peering at Lavender as if he could kill her right then and there.

She held up her finger, motioning for him to give her a minute while she was on the phone, and continued with her conversation as if he weren't there.

Rafiq slammed his fist down on the desk. "Get off the phone," he demanded, staring into her eyes like a pit bull ready to attack.

"What the hell is your problem?" Lavender, asked laying her phone on the desk.

"I know you heard me the first time. But since you wanna act slow today, I'm gonna humor you some. Why the *fuck* did you make Keon partner?"

"Because I wanted to," Lavender said, giving off a faint smile. She pulled out her nail file and started picking at her nails.

"He doesn't have a clue on how this place operates. I'm the one who stays here night after night balancing the books, doing payroll, and paying bills," Rafiq said, leaning over the desk toward Lavender. His nostrils flared. "That muthafucka just got here. What the fuck is your problem? I should have been partner, not him."

"Listen, Rafiq," Lavender said, choosing her words carefully. She could tell by the look on his face that he was about to snap. "Keon invested in the club with a hefty amount of cash. So that's why he's a partner."

Rafiq bit his bottom lip to stop him from saying anything else that he might regret later. He gave Lavender the nastiest look he could muster up. "You know what, Lav, it's cool. I ain't gonna even sweat that shit. I know that nigga could never run this club like I do." Rafiq started toward the door. His hand shook at he grabbed for the knob. He was scared that he was going to turn around and slap the shit out of Lavender for being such a bitch.

"It's nothing personal, Rafiq. Seriously, it was just business. Now if you'll excuse me, I need to make a phone call," Lavender said, putting her nail file down and picking up her phone. "Oh, Rafiq, I'm gonna need you to show Keon the ropes. He'll still be servicing clients but he still needs to learn how we operate."

Rafiq glanced at her as if she had just got off the short yellow school bus. "Fuck you," Rafiq mumbled, shutting the door to the office. He stormed down the hallway, praying to God that someone was stupid enough to get in his way so he could knock the shit out of them. Rafiq was starting to see his life deteriorate in front of his eyes. Usually, when things went wrong at work, he would go home to his wife and she would make everything okay. These days, he and his wife hardly ever talked, unless it was something regarding the kids. When Rafiq returned downstairs to the bar area, he poured himself two shots of Hennessy back to back and downed them both without so much as coming up for air. In Rafiq's eyes, Lavender was a backstabbing bitch. He didn't want to take it too far with Lavender this time because he knew that if she fired him again it would be for good, and Rafiq needed his job. He decided that he was just going to play along; at this point he had no other choice.

Rafiq let out the last few women from their interview group and returned to the bar area. They had been interviewing potential members all day and he was exhausted. It had been three weeks since they started the daunting task of recruiting new members, and since then he hadn't had a day off or made it home until after midnight. With the background checks and income verifications, he found himself swamped in paperwork daily. On top of it all, he still had to manage the daily operation of the club. And all Keon did was sit around and observe; at times he felt as though he was being spied on more than anything else. In Rafiq's mind, Lavender should have never made him partner. Yes, Keon was good with servicing the clients but he sucked at paperwork. He'd been trying to show him the paperwork system for almost a month now. Rafiq was starting to think he was a little slow; he just wasn't able to pick it up.

Rafiq sat beside Keon at the bar with the member applications and photos in front of him. He spaced them out so they could see each application individually. They looked over each of the applications carefully, looking for any little detail that would eliminate them from being eligible for membership. After sifting through about twenty applications, including salary verifications and education credentials, Rafiq and

Keon came up with seven eligible women. They could only potentially afford to take on five so they had to cut off two from the bunch.

"Here are the five I'm interested in," Rafiq said, pointing at the applications in front of them. "All of them have old money. They didn't just get a few couple of dollars and now they rich. Old money is good money," Rafiq said, folding his arms in front of him.

Keon scanned the photos and applications of the five women Rafiq was interested in and then shook his head. "Naw, man, I think I'm going to have to pass on this chick Madeline. She's sixty-five. You can say what you want but I know for a fact that my dick ain't gonna get hard for her. What about this one right here?" Keon said, pulling from one of the two applications Rafiq pushed to the side. "Toni Morales is her name. I think she would be a good candidate. She was real cool at her interview."

Rafiq's face scrunched up as he grabbed the application with her photo attached to the top out of Keon's hand. "This broad ain't got no real cake, man. According to her background checks and income verification she just became a millionaire over the past year. Plus she's only twenty-seven. Every member we have now is at least thirty-five."

"So—what's that mean?"

Rafiq let out a long sigh and then said, "It means that she is a potential risk. First of all, she is young. Most young people are emotionally unstable and unable to deal with the idea of just fucking someone without the feelings being involved. They say they can but they almost always wind up catching feelings. Most people who become millionaires lose their wealth within that first year. I swear, to be a partner you sure don't know much."

"Man, fuck you," Keon snapped. "This is who I want and as a partner"—he threw up his fingers and made the quotation signs—"my decision is final."

"Whatever," Rafiq said, sliding the applications in front of Keon. "Since your decision is final, you make the phone calls to them and let them know that they have been accepted. The new member brunch is scheduled for Sunday afternoon at three, so let them know that they need to be there. You think you can handle that?" Rafiq asked in a condescending tone.

"Yeah, man, I can handle that," Keon shot back, gathering all of the applications in one pile and placing them in a folder. He got up from the barstool and placed the folder under his arm. "I'll get at you lata. I got a client waiting on me."

"Yeah, a'ight," Rafiq said, returning to the other side of the bar.

There was no hiding the fact that Rafiq was still bitter about Keon being a partner. He tried his best to conceal his anger but his resentment always seemed to shine through. He decided that he was going to let Keon crash and burn. He would help him with what was necessary to keep the club afloat, but the other stuff he couldn't care less about. Rafiq was going to allow him to open and close the club from now on and play the role of an employee; he was going to work his eight hours and go home. He didn't care what went undone; it was the only way he could show Lavender how much of a big mistake she had made. He looked up at the clock; it was 7:00 P.M. His shift was just about over. He finished up behind the bar and grabbed his car keys from the shelf by the safe. He used a napkin to scribble a short message for Keon or Lavender, whichever of the two saw it first, letting them know that he would be leaving at seven from now on and was unavailable to work the weekends. Rafiq put his sunglasses on to shield him from the scorching summer sun and headed for the door. He didn't want to necessarily go home but he really had no other place to go. He'd made his family his life for so long that he really had no one to hang out with. Since he'd found out his wife was unfaithful, he really didn't have much to say to her. It had been well over a month and they never really had the conversation about why she did what she did. Rafiq wanted to know but, then again, he knew that he most likely would not be able to handle the details. No, he didn't catch them in "the act," but he wasn't stupid. The Magnum wrapper and used condom he found on the floor by the bed when he was cleaning up that night said it all. He got in the car and started on his journey home. He turned on the easy listening channel on his radio and took the longest route home he could find. All he could think about as he dipped throughout the neighborhoods in the city was where he went wrong with his wife and how to fix it.

Rafiq pulled up in the driveway and headed toward the house. He used the side door where the kitchen was located and went straight to the fridge to grab a cold beer.

"The police came to the house today," Farrah said, standing over the stove, stirring a pot of gumbo.

"What did they want?" Rafiq asked, leaning against the fridge with the beer in his hand. He used his teeth to pop the top off and took a gulp.

"They ask me about Edward," Farrah replied, opening the cabinet above the stove. She returned with a canister of creole spices and sprinkled them in the pot. "They asked me when was the last time I seen him."

"Ohhhhh, so that's his name, huh," Rafiq said, continuing to drink his beer. "And what did you tell them?"

"I told them that the last time I seen him was a month ago at spin class."

"So is that where you met homeboy from . . . the gym?"

"Yes." Farrah hesitated. "I met him at the gym."

"How long were you seeing him, Farrah?" Rafiq asked, clenching the beer bottle in his hand.

"Four months," she mumbled, continuing to focus on the pot of gumbo she was cooking.

"How many times did you fuck him, Farrah?" Rafiq asked drly.

"Twice, but I swear it was a mistake. I never meant to hurt you. I was lonely, Rafiq. You're never home; I'm always here alone with the kids and by the time you get in, it's so late that all we can do is go to sleep."

"Speaking of the kids, where are they anyway?"

"They're over my mom and dad's house for the week," she said, placing some peeled shrimp and onions in the pot, along with a clove of fresh garlic and cut up sausage pieces.

"Oh, okay," Rafiq said, taking another sip from his beer. "Did it seem like they bought it?" Rafiq asked, finishing off the beer and placing the empty bottle in the recycle bin on the side of the refrigerator.

"Yes, at least I think they did," Farrah said, continuing to add to the pot of gumbo, which was starting to simmer. "The one detective left his card. He told me to give him a call if he happens to call me or if I hear anything about his whereabouts."

Rafiq stood behind his wife and wrapped his arms around her body. He felt her body tense up as he hugged her tight and kissed her on the cheek. "Good job," he said, brushing her hair from her face. "How long before dinner will be ready?"

"It . . . it should be ready in about a half hour or so," Farrah stuttered.

"Good, good," Rafiq said, loosening his embrace. "I'll be in the family room watching TV if you need me." Rafiq left the kitchen and took a seat in the living room on the recliner. He pressed the lever to elevate his feet and flicked on the flat screen. That was the first time he touched his wife since that night. It was then that he realized that he still loved her, more than anything in the world. It would take some time for him to forgive her, but in due time all wounds were bound to heal. Besides, Rafiq had bigger fish to fry; the cops were bound to come back around and ask more questions at some point. As long as Farrah kept her mouth shut everything would be cool. Rafiq wasn't really concerned; he knew that he had Farrah so terrified of him that she would do anything to stay in his good graces. He wanted things to get better between them but, truth be told, he kind of liked her better like this; taking orders from him. For as long as he could remember he had done anything and everything in his power to make her happy. It felt good to be on the receiving end of the deal for a change and, as far as he was concerned, it could stay that way.

Chapter 16

And the Father Is . . .
Keon

Keon looked at the large vanilla envelope sitting on the coffee table with his name on it. He had been waiting over two weeks for the package to come and now that it arrived, he wasn't quite sure he was ready to open it. He took a seat on the couch and stared at it; wondering how the contents of the envelope would change his life forever. Keon took a deep breath and reached for it. He carefully ripped the envelope open, making sure that the letter was still intact. He pulled the one page letter from the envelope and read it. Tears flooded his eyes as he stuffed the letter back in the envelope and dropped it back on the coffee table. He wiped at his face as he grabbed his coat from the rack by the door and headed out.

Keon sat at the bar on Sixty-second and Lansdowne and sipped on a glass of Hennessy and Coke. He'd been there for an hour waiting for Chevy to arrive for her shift. After he told her that he didn't want anything to do with her even if the baby was his; she stopped returning his calls. The last time he spoke with her was three weeks ago when they took the paternity test. Now that Keon knew that Mariah was indeed his daughter,

he had to make amends; for his daughter's sake. He
hoped that Chevy was willing to allow him to be in her
life and understand at the same time that he didn't
want to be with her. Yes, Keon was lonely and wanted a
woman to call his own but just not her. Keon was a very
loyal person and once you lost his trust; that was it.

Keon grabbed Chevy's arm as soon as she walked
through the door. He gave her a fake smile and pulled
her back through the door so they could talk outside
the bar.

"I take it you got the results in the mail," Chevy said
folding her arms across her chest. "So . . . what did they
say?"

"You know what they said," Keon said, shoving his
hands in his pockets. "Listen, I just wanna be there for
my daughter. When can I see her?"

"So you ready to be a family now . . . huh," Chevy
said, sucking her teeth. "Now that you got the results
you wanna come crawling back."

"Now wait a minute," Keon said, throwing his hands
up in the air. "I just want to spend time with my daughter.
I'm not trying to be with you like that. I thought I made
that clear to you when the dude Tim came to my crib."

Chevy rolled her eyes and then said, "Me and her
come as a package deal. So if you not trying to be a family then you not trying to see your daughter."

"Come on with the dumb shit Chev," Keon said,
raising his voice. He was usually calm but she was out
of line and Keon wasn't about to give up his daughter
because she couldn't handle the fact that he just wasn't
interested in her anymore. "I don't want to have to take
you to court Chevy."

She looked over at him and burst out in laughter,
"Nigga please, take me to court? Are you sure you want
to do that? Once they find out what you really do at that

club you won't have to worry about ever seeing Mariah again. Your ass gonna be back upstate so fast that your cot still gonna be warm."

"What the fuck are you talking about?" Looking at Chevy as if he could ring her neck. "I'm a fucking janitor, ain't nobody goin' upstate."

"You must really think I'm stupid K," Chevy said, shaking her head. "Everybody around the way knows you out here fucking bitches for money. What you think I wasn't gonna find out? You know that nigga Marquise can't keep his mouth shut for shit. All it took was for him to tell one person and now everybody knows. I suggest you make your decision; It's either me and Mariah or nothing at all. Call me when you ready to let me know what it's hittin' for." Chevy took one last look at Keon and waltzed back in the bar.

Keon could feel his body getting hot; he rushed over to the door and kicked it as hard as he could, causing the bottom glass to shatter. All he wanted to do was be a responsible father and take care of his child. He hurried up the street and dissapperared around the corner before anyone called the police. He knew Marquise was going to run his mouth; it was in his nature. He gossiped like a girl but he was loyal and had looked out of Keon when he was locked up. He just didn't expect everyone to know his business. He didn't really care; he just didn't want it to get back to his PO. That's why Keon was so determined to save enough money to open his own business. Then, no-one would have anything to say about what he did for a living.

He knew that he wasn't in the position to fight Chevy for custody so he decided to just fall back. It pained him to think about not being able to see his daughter like he wanted to but he had no other choice. He hoped that at some point Chevy would change her mind but he knew that it was going to take some time. He continued his walk home, dipping through small streets as a precaution; just in case the police was looking for him for busting the door. He hadn't felt that mad in a while. Chevy always knew how to push his buttons and take him over the edge. She could be a real bitch and she was going to give him a run for his money. As he laid down in bed that night, he said a quick prayer; something he hadn't done since he got out of prision. He asked God to allow him to be the good father he knew he could be to his daughter

Keon, threw the pillow over his head as the door bell continued ringing for the tenth time in a row. He peeked from under his comforter at the digital clock on his dresser; it was eight am on a Saturday morning. He wasn't expecting anyone and figured that most likely it was the Jehovah's Witnesses out spreading the word. He continued to lie in bed hoping that they would get the point and go away.

"Keon," his grandmother yelled from the bottom of the steps. "Come get the door. It's for you."

Keon flung the comforter off in frustration and sat up in the bed. This was his first weekend off in four months and he planned on sleeping in. He reached over the side of the bed and grabbed a t-shirt from the floor. He slipped on his Nike shower slides and headed down stairs. He paused when he got to the steps; he noticed Chevy standing at the bottom holding Mariah's hand. Keon continued down the steps and motioned for her to follow him over to the couch.

"What's up? Everything cool?" Keon asked, looking at her with heartfelt eyes. He could tell she had something on her mind; her eyes were red as if she's been crying all night.

"I've been thinking," Chevy said, clearing her throat. "I want to apologize for what I said to you yesterday at the bar. I don't want to be that type of woman. You know the type that uses her child as a pawn to control a man. My mother was like that with my father. He stayed with us for a few years but once he really got tired of her, he left and we never heard from him again. Mariah deserves a father whether we're together or not."

Keon leaned back on the couch and folded his hands in his lap; he was speechless. He continued to remain quiet as she finished talking.

"I want you to start getting her on your days off and any other time you want to spend time with her. I love you Keon, I always did. I might not have always made the best choices when it came to our relationship but I always had good intentions. I never loved Tim; he was simply a filler to pay the bills. I was down and out and I needed money to send Mariah to daycare. He was feelin' me so we got together and he took care of me and my baby. I never meant to hurt you Keon, I really didn't." Chevy said, wiping her eyes with the sleeve of her wool pea coat.

Keon grabbed her close and kissed her on the forehead, "I'm sorry things didn't work out between us. Let's just be the best parents we can be to Mariah."

"I can agree to that," Chevy said, lying her head on his shoulder.

"Good, good," Keon said, brushing her hair out of his face. "I'm glad we were able to work everything out. I really missed my baby." He picked Mariah up and sat her on his lap. He hugged her tight, as if he was never going to let go. "Since your both here, how about some breakfast?" he asked, getting up from the couch and carrying Mariah over to the kitchen table. He pulled

the seat out across from his grandmother who was finishing up her morning tea and sat her in it.

"I thought you'd never ask," Chevy said following
behind him.

Chapter 17

Breakin' All the Rules
Keon

Keon sat at the bar and puffed on a cigar as he waited for his next appointment to arrive. He'd already serviced five members so far and this would make his last for the day. It was 10:00 P.M. and, if he played it right, he would be done by midnight. He reached over and grabbed the appointment book from behind the counter. He scanned through to see who was up next; it was the chick Toni Morales. He quickly placed the half-smoked cigar in the ashtray and placed the book back where it belonged. He looked over at Lavender; she was cleaning up behind the bar.

"Hey, Lav, I'm going upstairs to get ready for my last appointment. You can just send her up when she arrives—no need to buzz me, okay?"

"Will do," Lavender said dryly. "Listen, you mind closing after you're done? I'm really tired and I need to get some sleep."

"Not a problem, just let her in and leave whenever you're ready." He could tell that Lavender was tired of working in the evenings, but ever since Rafiq started leaving at seven, she had no choice. He headed up to his room and took a nice long, hot shower. He dried off and wrapped the towel around his waist. When he returned to his room, Toni was sitting in the chair in the corner smiling like the Cheshire cat.

"Hey, I didn't hear you come in," Keon said, trying not to stare. He couldn't help but notice her hardened nipples protruding though her white spaghetti-strap tank top.

"I'm sorry I startled you," Toni said after clearing her throat. "Lavender told me it was okay to come right up."

"Don't worry about it, it's cool. I was just freshening up a bit," Keon said, avoiding eye contact. "So . . . we can get down to business . . . if you like."

"Of course," Toni said, then cleared her throat again in nervousness. She stood up from the chair and started to pull her shirt over her head.

"Wait a minute," Keon said, rushing over to her. "I can help you with that." He pulled the shirt over her head and kissed her softly on the shoulder. He brushed her hair to the side and planted his lips on her neck, swirling his tongue around while kissing her softly.

Toni backed away and looked at Keon. Her face was flustered; it was obvious that she was nervous. "Can we just chill for a minute?" she asked, taking a seat back in the recliner. She picked her shirt back up from the floor and held it in her lap. "So, how was your day?" she asked, trying to regain her composure.

"How was my day?" Keon looked confused. No one had ever asked him that before. Well, at least no client ever did. "I guess it was cool . . . For the most part I've been at work. So how was your day?" Keon asked. He took a seat on the side of the bed by the recliner, where Toni was sitting.

"I'm a little tired. My back and neck hurt. I've been in meetings all day," she said, kicking off her heels and rubbing her foot. "I swear I need a massage."

"No problem," Keon said, jumping up from the bed and rushing over to the dresser. He returned with a bottle of massage oil and a porcupine massage ball. He grabbed her by the hand and led her toward the bed. "Lie down," he said.. Keon opened the oil and poured a nice-sized amount on the small of her back, and rubbed up and down, paying special attention to the tightness in her shoulders.

"So tell me about yourself . . . I mean, how long have you been working here?"

"Not that long . . . for a few months now," Keon said, continuing to rub her down.

"Do you like it?"

"It's okay, I guess. The money is good," Keon replied, pouring more oil on her back and rubbing it in. "It's not really what I want to do with my life but, you know, you gotta do what you have to in order to survive out here."

"So what do you really want to do then? I'm a firm believer that if you have a dream you should try your best to live it."

Keon begin yapping away, telling her about his dreams to open a janitorial service, forgetting all about the club rule about sharing personal business. From there, he talked about his daughter Mariah and how proud he was to be a father. It had been so long since a woman had shown real interest in him that he was actually enjoying his time with her. Before he knew it, it was almost midnight and they didn't even have sex yet. Appointments usually only lasted for two hours and she was nearing the end of hers.

"This feels so good," Toni moaned. "Thank you so much."

"You're welcome," Keon said, feeling a bit awkward. None of his clients ever thanked him for his services. "Well, it's midnight and we didn't get to have sex. Would you like me to have Lavender refund your money? We usually don't do refunds but in this case I'm sure she wouldn't mind."

"Refund? I don't need a refund. I enjoyed my time with you . . . without the sex."

"You sure?" Keon asked, scratching his head.

"Real sure," Toni said. "Now, do you mind if I do you?" Toni asked, sitting up from the bed and grasping the bottle of massage oil in her hand.

"If you want," Keon said, shrugging his shoulders.

"Lie down," she said, mimicking what Keon told her earlier.

Keon did as instructed and took her place on the bed. He closed his eyes and listened to her tell him about her childhood and what it was like living in a family full of boys and how she was big-boned growing up. Keon hadn't had a good conversation in such a long time that he found himself revealing more and more things about himself. Before he knew it the sun was coming up. He looked over at the clock and it was 5:00 A.M. They'd spent the entire night talking to each other and he wasn't even sleepy. It wasn't until she left that he realized he'd made a major mistake. She knew his real name and almost everything there was to know about him—everything except where he lived, that is. She was just so easy to talk to; her sultry voice caused him to become relaxed and put his guard down.

Keon decided there was no reason for him to go home now. He might as well stay until tonight when his shift was over at the club. On one hand, he felt foolish for giving up so much information, but on the other, he wished he had someone to talk to like that all the time. It still surprised him that she didn't want a refund. Keon knew that he was treading in dangerous waters so he decided the next time he and Toni crossed paths, he would keep it strictly business.

When Keon got home that night, he found his grandmother sitting on the front porch, waiting for him. He thought he was seeing things at first because when he looked at his watch when he got out of the cab, it said 1:00 A.M., and his grandmother barely could stay awake during her game shows at night.

"Hey Big Ma, what you doing up?" Keon asked, walking up the front steps to the porch.

"Your parole officer and them just left here. They was in here searching the house, saying they have reason to believe that you're engaging in illegal activity," she said, peering over her glasses. "Do you know what they hell they talking 'bout? Keon, you better not be doing nothing stupid out there in them streets. You know if you go back this time you ain't coming home for a long time. They turned my house upside down looking for whatever they could find. You know they had the nerve to pour my coffee grounds out, talking 'bout you could have hid something in there. You know I likes my coffee in the morning. Now I'm all out."

Keon searched his mind, trying to recall even the slightest detail that would cause his parole office to think he was doing something out of pocket. He didn't even call Keon and tell him he was coming out. Besides, he knew Keon worked well into the morning hours almost nightly so he didn't understand why he would raid the house. Plus, he just went and saw him yesterday to check in, take a pee test, and provide monthly paystubs; everything was cool then. "Big Ma, I swear I ain't doing nothing illegal. I'm at work almost every day and when I'm not I'm home. I'm going to call my probation office in the morning to find out what the hell is going on."

"I swear, Keon, if I find out you lying to me and you out there in them streets again, my heart is gonna be broken. You promised me you was gonna come out here and do the right thing and I'm going to hold you to it," Big Ma said. "Plus you got that baby now. You gotta step up and be a man and stop getting yourself in trouble. That little girl needs you cause Lawd knows that mother of hers ain't got no sense." She used her cane as a support to get up from the porch chair. "I'm going to bed, baby," she said, opening the screen door and disappearing up the steps.

Keon took a seat on the porch in the same chair that his grandmother just got up from and buried his face in his hands. He was too close to ending his parole for shit like this to happen. He had friends but he rarely talked to them. The only person he used to really hang with was Marquise and that nigga was locked up. He decided he wasn't going to keep racking his brain regarding the matter and that he was going to go inside to get some sleep.

Keon jumped up from the seat as if he had seen a ghost; he ran upstairs to his room to check his stash. With the type of money he was bringing in at the club, there was no way he could put the money in the bank; instead, he hid it in his room. He burst through his bedroom door to find the mattress flipped up and the contents of his dresser drawers lying in small piles around the room. He stepped over the mess that covered his floor and headed straight toward the closet. The door to the closet was wide open and the top shelf was bare; all the sneaker boxes that contained his porno videos and magazines where now dumped at the bottom of his closet. His clothes hung off the hangers and were pushed to the side. He rummaged through the pile at the bottom of his closet until he reached the back. He felt around in the corner for the little metal box where he kept his money and basketball cards and pulled it out; the lock was popped. He opened it up and it was empty. Keon threw the box across the room; it hit the wall, causing a loud thump before it hit the floor.

"*Fuck,*" Keon yelled, getting on his hands and knees to search the back of the closet in hopes that it may have fallen back there. All of the money that he earned during his time at the club was gone. There was no way he'd be able to make that type of money back now. The only money that was left sat in his pants pocket. Keon sat against the closet wall and hit his head against it. Tears welled up in his eyes as he thought about having to start saving money all over again.

When Keon woke up the next day, it was already one P.M. He'd slept well through the morning and was running late for work. He quickly dialed the club and waited for someone to answer.

"Good afternoon," Rafiq sang into the phone.

"Hey, Rafiq, it's me, Keon. I'm running late. I overslept."

"Wrong day to oversleep, buddy," Rafiq said, turning his back away from the bar. "Your parole officer is here waiting on you. He keeps asking weird questions about what you do here, like he doesn't already know. Is something going on that I need to know?"

"Naw, I don't know why the bull on my back all of a sudden," Keon said, rushing around the room, looking for some clothes to put on. "Listen, I should be there in about an hour."

"Just hurry up. I don't want him to start looking around. I called the boys and ceased all activity until he leaves. We're losing money . . . so the faster you get here the better," Rafiq whispered, looking behind him; his eyes instantly met with the parole officer's. Rafiq gave off a quick smile and turned back around.

"I got you. I'm on my way," Keon said, hopping on one foot as he tried to put his sneaker on. He hung up the phone and jetted down the steps and out of the house so fast that he didn't even get a chance to say good-bye to his grandmother. He rushed down to the avenue and caught the first hack he could find. He paid the hack man fifty dollars to get him there as fast as he could. When Keon looked up, he was pulling into the parking lot of the club; he made it there in less than thirty minutes. He grabbed his duffel bag from the seat beside him and made his way to the door. He raised his hand to knock and before he could do so, the door flung open.

"Keon," Rafiq said, giving him the eye to let him know the parole officer was right behind him. "Thanks for calling us to let us know you were going to be late."

"I'm sorry," Keon apologized, closing the door behind him. "I was here late buffing floors last night and I overslept."

"It's quite all right," Rafiq said, returning to the other side of the bar. "You can start upstairs today with the bathrooms."

"Sure, not a problem," Keon said, walking toward the supply closet like he was about to start working.

"Keon, I need to speak with you for a moment," the parole officer said, walking up behind him.

"Oh, hey, Mr. Thompson, what are you doing here?" Keon asked, acting as if he didn't know he was there.

"I came to check up on you. Can we have a word?" he said, motioning for him to step away from the supply closet.

"Sure, sure. What's up?" Keon said, stepping away from the supply closet and leaning against the wall across from it.

"I've been hearing some things about you, Keon . . . not-so-good things . . . I just wanted you to know that I'm going to be watching you. When you get in at night, I want you to call my cell phone to check in. I want you in my office every week for drug testing. And, lastly, just know that I'll be doing more pop-up visits; here and at home. So be prepared."

"I don't understand . . . What did I do?"

"Just watch yourself, son. I don't want to see you wind up back in the pen," Thompson said, patting Keon on the shoulder.

"What did I do?' Keon repeated, staring at his parole officer as he walked away.

Mr. Thompson walked off toward the bar area, ignoring Keon's question for a second time. He stopped at the front door and waited for Rafiq to let him out.

"What was that all about?" Rafiq asked, walking over toward Keon, who was still standing by the janitor's closet.

"I don't know, man, he trippin'. I swear I ain't done shit. I've been keeping my nose clean. I don't know why he on my back all heavy and shit. Them niggas ran up in my crib last night. They took my stash; I'm fuckin' broke, man. I'm gonna be working at this club forever trying to make that money back."

"Damn, homie, what you gonna do?" Rafiq said, trying to conceal his satisfaction. Rafiq bit his lip in hopes of masking the smile that just couldn't help but keep trying to break through.

"I don't know, man—I just don't know," Keon said, shaking his head.

For the next month, Keon worked nonstop without any days off. He took as many appointments as his schedule allowed and worked his ass off for tips. Keon no longer kept money at home but, instead, left it in his room in a small slit in his mattress. He kept no more than $200 at a time on him; that way if the law ran up on him there wasn't much they would find. Keon's parole officer was still down his neck like a fire-breathing dragon. He was getting so tired of checking in with him daily that he was starting to think that it was just easier to go back to jail.

He and Toni saw each other at least twice a week, and during those meetings they never once had sex. Instead, they laughed, joked, and continued to tell each other personal stories about their lives. Keon's guilt about breaking club rules went out the window. The companionship he was getting from Toni was like something he had never had before and he was really starting to feel her. He looked forward to their sessions and often found himself thinking about her and what it would be like to make love to her. He was starting to wonder if she was a lesbian because although she claimed she liked guys, she never made a move on him. He'd tried to get close to her a few times and she shied away. Nonetheless, Keon had fallen for her, hard. She was perfect for him, despite the fact that she was a client and all. She made him feel good and she liked him for who he was. And in Keon's eyes that was well worth the risk.

Chapter 18

Boy Toy
Lavender

Lavender pulled over on the side of the dirt road and turned her car off. She rolled her window down halfway and then said, "How are you tonight, Officer?"

"License and registration," the police officer said, beaming his flashlight in Lavender's face.

Lavender reached over to the glove compartment and returned with the documents. She placed them in the officer's hand and then said, "Why am I being stopped, Officer?"

"Miss, are you serious?" the police officer asked, looking at her like she was crazy. "You were swerving all over the road. I followed you for two blocks with my lights on and you're just pulling over."

"Two blocks?" Lavender said. "That can't be right. I didn't see any lights."

"Maybe because you were too busy over there smoking your joint," he said, glancing at the package of E-Z Wider and the dime bag of weed sitting on the passenger seat.

Lavender fixated her eyes on the officer, giving off a look that translated that she was willing to do whatever it took not to get locked up. "I'm sorry, Officer. My boyfriend left that stuff in my car. I just dropped him off; that's where I was coming from."

"Get out of the car," the officer demanded, ignoring her advances. "And place your hands on the hood."

Lavender swung her feet around the side of the car and stood up; her four-inch heels allowed her to come face to face with the officer. She pranced around the side of the car and placed her hands on the hood as instructed.

The officer kept on eye on Lavender while he searched the car. When he was finished, he found two more dime bags and a Ziploc bag full of yellow pills. "I'm going to have to take you in, ma'am," he said, unhooking his cuffs from his belt.

"Please, Officer, don't arrest me. I'll do anything," Lavender pleaded. "I told you I let my boyfriend hold my car. I swear to you I didn't know all the stuff was in there."

"Come on now, miss, you're trying to tell me that you wasn't smoking marijuana? First off, your eyes are red and glassy as hell; secondly, I seen you ditch the joint out the window when you were pulling over," he said, grabbing her wrists and placing them behind her back.

"Yes, I was smoking a joint," Lavender admitted, "but the other stuff isn't mines. The only reason I was smoking it was because I seen it in the ashtray. I swear, Officer, my boyfriend had my car all day. I'm just leaving his house now."

"Where does this boyfriend of yours live?" the officer asked, walking her over to the car in handcuffs. He opened the door and pushed her head down so she could get inside.

Without thinking, Lavender blurted out Keon's entire government name and address. She watched as the officer called in and repeated the information to the dispatcher, sending a car over to his house.

"So, you're really going to take me to jail?" Lavender asked, looking concerned. "I gave you his information."

"I sure am, sweetheart. Tell it to the judge and let's see if he believes you," the officer said, pulling off.

Lavender already had it in her mind that she would use her one phone call to contact Benjamin, her old client. He was a well-respected judge in the city and had gotten her out of trouble on several occasions. She made sure to make herself a mental note to clear Keon from any trouble she may have caused by using him as a scapegoat as well. Lavender already figured they were going to go and search his house; she could tell by the conversation the officer was having through the radio.

Lavender was out of jail by the next morning; one quick call to the judge and fifteen minutes later, she was released. After three hours at the impound trying to retrieve her car, Lavender was finally on her way home. Once in the door, Lavender headed straight to the shower to get dressed for work. It was almost three P.M. and she was nowhere ready to walk out the door. With a towel wrapped around her body and one wrapped around her head she stood in front of her closet and eyed her selections. She chose a cute little minidress from Bebe. She took it off the rack and slipped it on; when Lavender looked in the mirror, she almost screamed. Her once flat stomach now donned a little pouch. Lavender quickly slid it off as fast as she had put it on.

She already knew what her problem was: she'd been eating like a pig. She'd substituted her snorting for smoking weed and she was always sleepy and hungry. Although they were altogether different highs, as long as she was high she didn't care. Lavender searched her closet again and found a fuchsia-colored maxi dress. She pulled it over her head and it fell to the floor, hiding any evidence of her protruding tummy. She slipped on a pair of Tory Burch platform sandals that wrapped around her ankles. Lavender applied her makeup and picked at her hair; her signature china doll weave was shining without a hair out of place. She covered her eyes with a pair of gold Gucci aviators, grabbed her purse from the hallway table and headed for the door. She could hear the cell phone ringing in her bag; she didn't bother to answer. She already knew it was probably Rafiq asking where the hell she was.

Lavender left the building and headed toward her car. She got in and dug around in her purse for her secret stash of marijuana and rolled herself a joint. Lavender used the cigarette lighter in the car and blazed up. She puffed away on her joint and made the short trip from her home to the club. Lavender had been smoking weed now for over two months, and even though it didn't energize her like her other drug of choice, it got the job done. She was roasted most of the day, using her drive to and from work as times to get high. Weed was much cheaper than coke and she didn't need to smoke as much as she snorted. Once she was high off weed, she was high for hours at a time.

When Lavender arrived at the club, she found Keon and Rafiq sitting at the bar, chatting as if they were best friends. She knew that they were getting along better but she had never seen them laughing and joking before.

"Hey, what's going on?" Lavender asked, taking a seat on the side of Keon.

"Nothing much," Keon said, glancing over at Rafiq and then at Lavender. "What's been up with you?"

"Yeah, why are you so late anyway?" Rafiq asked, getting up from the stool and heading toward the other side of the bar.

"I had a long night," Lavender said, removing her sunglasses and placing them on the bar.

"What, somebody wear that ass out?" Keon joked, looking at Lavender as if she were a slab of ribs at a cookout.

"Now, K, you and I both know that you're the only one wearin' this ass out." Lavender smirked. "You know you're my man."

Keon let out a chuckle and then said, "You can get it all day from over here."

Rafiq rolled his eyes. "What you drinkin', Lav?"

"Can I get a mimosa?" she asked, plopping her bag on the stool beside her.

Rafiq whizzed around the bar, pouring Lavender's drink and placing it in front of her on a coaster. He then returned to the other side of the bar and took a seat.

"So how's business? It looks a little light in here," Lavender asked, looking around the club. There were two clients on the floor waiting to get serviced.

"We've made about ten grand since we opened," Rafiq said, reaching over the bar and grabbing the book. He flipped it open and looked at the remaining appointments for the day. "We should make our daily quota. Keon here has a double block with Toni tonight . . . That should seal the deal and top us off at fifty grand for the day."

"Double block, huh?" Lavender said, taking a sip of mimosa and placing the glass back down in front of her. "You been seeing that chick Toni a lot lately." Lavender glanced over at Keon.

Rafiq grinned as he got up from the stool and went to check on the clients who were waiting to be serviced.

Keon shot him a dirty look and then turned to Lavender. "Yeah, I guess she like the way I be dickin' her down."

"Let me find out she getting more dick that I am." Lavender pouted, folding her arms across her chest like a two-year-old child.

"She pay, Lav, you don't . . . anymore . . . That's the difference," Keon said, finishing off a can of Red Bull.

"You coming over tonight?" Lavender asked, staring at the side of his face, trying her best to make him feel uncomfortable.

"I can't, Lav . . . Remember, my PO on my back. I gotta go straight home from work."

"How 'bout if I come to your house?" Lavender said, taking another sip of her drink.

"I don't know about that . . . By the time I'm done tonight I'ma be tired as shit."

"Why you making excuses? Any other time you game. What's the difference now?" Lavender said, raising her voice in a manner that caused the clients and Rafiq to stop talking and turn around to see what was going on.

Keon looked over at the clients and gave off a warm smile, and then turned back to Lavender. "Listen, Lav, not tonight. Maybe some other time," Keon said through clenched teeth. "Now if you'll excuse me, I gotta go get ready for my next appointment." Keon tossed the empty can of Red Bull across the bar and into the trash can. He took one last look at Lavender and walked off, heading toward the second floor.

This was the third time in a row that Keon had turned Lavender down when she wanted some and she did not like it. Lavender had a feeling that he was seeing someone, another woman. No, they never established the fact that they were together, but in Lavender's mind it was written the day she let him hit raw. He did tell her on several occasions that she was special to him and that she was the only woman he was fucking outside the club. So, she took that as them being together. Plus, she had stayed over at his house many a night and had also met his grandmother. Something fishy was going on and she was going to get to the bottom of it. Before he became partner, they were fucking like two teenagers, and now she could barely get his attention. She finished off her drink and got up from the bar. She grabbed her shades and bag from the bar and headed upstairs to her office. Once inside, she dumped everything on her desk and plopped down in the chair. She spun around slowly, thinking of reasons as to why Keon was acting so strange. She recalled the words that came out of Rafiq's mouth about Keon having a double block session with the one client Toni, and rushed downstairs to grab the appointment book. She sat at the bar and opened the book and looked back two weeks to see how many times he had met with her. According to Lavender's count, Keon had over six sessions with her.

"What you looking at?" Rafiq said, walking back over to the bar from the lounge area.

"Nothing, just browsing the appointment book," Lavender said nonchalantly.

"Browsing for what?" Rafiq said, standing over her shoulder.

Lavender closed the book and gave a fake smile. "So . . . Rafiq, don't you think it's strange that Keon and the new client Toni has had about six sessions in the last two weeks?"

"Strange?" Rafiq repeated, cutting his eyes her way. "Nah, not at all. When Ming was still a client she met with Keon five days straight. They say he is the best at what he does. And from the way you're acting . . . I can see that's an understatement. I ain't never seen you trip like this over some dick. What's gotten into you, anyway?"

"Forget it," Lavender said, copping an attitude. She slammed the book shut and left it on the counter. Lavender huffed and puffed as she made her way back up to her office. As she rounded the hallway, Toni was entering Keon's room to be serviced. They locked eyes as they passed each other; Lavender didn't even bother to greet her. Lavender looked back down the hall after she passed; she had a sort of waddle to her like a fat girl. There was something about her that made Lavender want to grab her by the hair and drag her down the stairs face down. Lavender was going to keep a close eye on Toni and Keon. He was her boy toy and she wasn't going to let Toni or anyone else change that.

Chapter 19

In Love with a Client
Keon

Keon sprayed Issey Miyake on the back of his neck and under his arms, preparing for his next client. He already knew Toni was next on the appointment book and he wanted to make sure that he was looking and smelling good. He looked in the mirror at his reflection; he had bags under his eyes large enough to carry fifty dollars worth of groceries. Keon was dog tired. For the last three months, he was opening and closing the club daily as well as servicing clients. But according to his calculations, business was better than it had ever been. Since they took on the five new members three months ago, revenue more than doubled; every employee saw at least a grand more on their check a week and company morale was through the roof. If he played it right, he could be done with the club in as little as three months.

Once he was finished being a "working man" he saw no reason why he couldn't be in a relationship with Toni, and was hoping that maybe they could start a life together. He opened the bedside table drawer and inside was a small satin box. He removed it and opened it up; inside lay a two-carat, princess-cut diamond ring. Keon knew he was being a little forward thinking about asking Toni to marry him but he didn't care; he was in love. She was everything he ever wanted in a woman and, club or no club, he just couldn't let that slip away from him.

Keon hurried and placed the box back in the drawer as he heard a faint knock at his bedroom door. He reached for the knob and opened it; Toni was standing in the doorway with a seductive grin on her face. He pulled her inside by her waist and slammed the door shut.

"Strip for me," Keon said, pulling away and taking a seat on the bed.

Toni nodded and started unbuttoning her blouse.

Keon had finally waxed that ass two weeks ago and, boy, was the wait well worth it. Her pussy was so tight that Keon had no doubt in his mind that she was a virgin. But ever since then, they'd been fucking like jackrabbits. Keon loved the fact that she couldn't get enough of him. Yes, he had other clients like that, but Toni was different. They had waited so long to have sex that Keon knew she just didn't want him for his body. Keon grabbed Toni and threw her down on the bed. He turned the lights off and went to work.

Two hours later, Keon turned the lamp back on and looked at Toni; her hair was all over her head. Keon kissed her on the forehead and picked his boxers up from the floor and slid them on. He headed toward the bathroom to wash up before his next appointment.

"I was thinking," Toni said, gathering her clothes from the pile beside the bed. "Why don't we get together, you know . . . outside the club."

"You know we can't do that," Keon said, peeking out of the bathroom with his toothbrush in his mouth. "It's against club rules."

"I know, I know, but I figured it would be nice . . . you know . . . you and I . . . chillin' together, watching a movie or something. You said you wish we could hang out outside the club. No one has to know. It's not like we're going out on a date or something. We'll be in the house, behind closed doors."

"I don't know about that," Keon said, returning to the sink to rinse the toothpaste out of his mouth. "It's too risky."

Even though Keon loved Toni, he wasn't ready to take their relationship outside the club. He still had crazy Lavender to think about. She was starting to pop up at his grandmother's house all the time and he didn't want to chance them running into each other. He still hadn't figured out a way to ease away from Lavender, and it was hard to turn her down when she wanted to fuck. She took it personal, and for the time being he had to play along, because he needed his job and he invested too much money in to it to have Lavender and him beefin'. So when she wanted to fuck, he gave her the dick without any issues, whether she was paying or not.

"I don't see how," Toni said, getting snappy. "We already talk on the phone—almost every day. That's against the club rules, ain't it? So what would be the difference?"

"The difference is that someone might see us outside the club and I could lose my job," Keon said. "Then how the hell am I gonna start my business?"

"I can help you start your business," Toni said, slipping back into her clothes. "I'm just tired of hiding my love for you inside this place."

"Love . . . for me . . . huh," Keon said, dipping his head out of the bathroom door. "So what you trying to say?"

"I'm trying to say that I love you and I want to be with you outside the club," Toni admitted, sitting on the bed and slipping on her heels.

Keon's heart thudded; he had never heard any woman, not even his mother, tell him she loved him. "Okay, okay, your place or mines?" Keon asked, walking out of the bathroom with a towel on his shoulder.

"Yours," Toni said, jumping up from the bed and wrapping her hands around his shoulders.

Keon packed his duffel bag and prepared himself for his trip home. It was almost ten P.M. and he promised Toni that she could spend the night with him tonight. He wanted to get home so he could tidy up his room before she arrived. He was kind of nervous about her seeing where he lived, and it didn't help that he stayed with his grandmother. He hoped that she was asleep when she got in so she wouldn't be asking a lot of questions about his guest. He zipped up his bag and locked the door to his room. He started down the steps with his hands in his pockets and as soon as he reached the front door, Lavender pulled his arm.

"What's up for tonight?" Lavender asked, licking her lips as if Keon was a T-bone steak.

"Nothing," Keon stuttered, trying to avoid eye contact. Lavender had a habit of staring a nigga down so bad that she could see in your soul. Keon didn't want to give her a reason to think that he was lying; otherwise, he knew she was going to show up at his crib whether he liked it or not. "My grandma is sick. So I'm gonna go home and make sure she a'ight."

Lavender sucked her teeth and then said, "Damn, I was looking forward to you wearing this ass out tonight."

"I got you, babe, another time," Keon said, kissing her on the cheek.

He took a deep breath and headed out the door, hoping that she wouldn't stop him again.

Keon cuddled up to Toni and flicked on the TV. He surfed the channels until he came across the movie *Halloween*. It felt so good to be in her presence outside the club that Keon was almost ready to quit right then and there. Keon heard a horn blowing. He got up from the couch and looked outside the curtain; there were car lights flashing on and off across the street. It looked like Lavender's cherry red BMW.

"I'll be right back," Keon said, grabbing his hoodie from the rack and heading out the door. He made his way across the street, and just as he thought, it was Lavender sitting in the driver's seat.

She rolled the window down and grabbed at his jeans. "Hey, K, what's up?"

"What are you doing here, Lav? I told you my grandma sick," Keon said, looking at her eyes. They were glazed over, so Keon instantly knew she had been getting high.

"I figured we could at least get a quickie in the car," Lavender said, smiling deviously.

"Naw, I'm not doing that," Keon said, looking at her like she had lost her mind. "Take your ass home, man, you know I don't like fuckin' with you when you high anyway."

"Come on," Lavender whined. "I'm horny. I need some dick . . . bad."

"I said go home, Lav," Keon said, swatting her wandering hand away. "I'll get at you tomorrow if she feeling better."

Lavender rolled her eyes and then looked past Keon to the silver-colored Mercedes parked in front of his house. "Whose car is that?" Lavender asked, pointing to the car.

Keon looked over at the car to see what she was talking about; it was Toni's car. "I don't know, maybe it's one of the neighbors."

Lavender stared at Keon for a minute as if she knew that he was lying, and then said, "Promise me we're going to get together tomorrow. I can't wait any longer."

"Okay, Okay, I promise," Keon said, hoping that Lavender would just leave. "Scout's honor." He threw up his two fingers.

"See you tomorrow," Lavender said, grabbing at his crotch once more.

Keon stood in the street and watched as Lavender drove off and turned the corner. He then ran back in the house to find Toni sitting on the couch with her arms folded.

"Who was that?" Toni huffed.

"That was Lavender. She locked herself out of the club so I had to give her mines," Keon said, sitting back down on the couch and placing his arm around her. He pulled her close to him and brushed her hair away from her ear. "I love you too," he whispered. "I love you too."

Chapter 20

Old Habits Die Hard
Lavender

Lavender sat at her desk and reached in the drawer for the crystallized candy jar where she kept her stash. She purchased a new dish a few weeks ago when she got the itch to start snorting again. She scooped up a small amount with her pinky finger. She held her nostril and inhaled; she repeated the action twice more. Lavender closed her eyes and thought about the last time she and Keon made love. It was rougher than she had ever had it in her life. She couldn't wait until he came in today; she was going to clear her desk off and lie on top of it spread-eagle. She jumped up from her chair and ran downstairs to check the appointment book to see what time he would be in.

She scanned down to his name; he was due in at noon and his first appointment was the girl Toni. Lavender was getting sick and tired of seeing her in his appointment book. She used a red pen to cross her name out. She moved Toni to King, another one of their employees. If Lavender saw that a certain client was spending too much time with one employee, she banned them from seeing them from two weeks to a month. It was sort of a way to get them to try something new. It kept people from getting serious and breaking club rules in the long run. She hadn't done it in a while but she could exercise the right at any time; it was in the client handbook.

Lavender whizzed around the bar, preparing for the opening of the club. She hummed as she stocked the shelves, put the glasses up, and emptied all the ashtrays. She loved the feeling she was having; she was upbeat and got tasks done fast and she owed it all to her snorting again. Weed was doing nothing but making her fat, tired, and hungry, and in Lavender's line of work, none of those were appealing. It had only been two weeks since she started snorting again and she already lost fifteen pounds. Her body looked better than ever and she felt better than ever. After she finished balancing the books and counting the safe, she sat down at the bar with a glass of mimosa in front of her and waited for the guys to arrive. Lavender opened and closed the door as each one trickled in. Right before start time, Keon pressed the buzzer and she got up to answer as she did all the other times.

"What's up, K," Lavender said, moving to the side so he could get in. She noticed the girl Toni pulling up in the parking lot and she closed the door all the same.

"Nothin', chillin'," Keon said, dumping his duffel bag on the floor and taking a seat at the bar. "Can you grab me a can of Red Bull?"

"Sure," Lavender said, ignoring the buzzer at the door as she made her way to the refrigerator to grab Keon's drink. "You want this straight or you want it mixed with a little Henny?"

"Naw, just the Red Bull. My PO been on my ass. I can drink no alcohol. He just sittin' waitin' for me to fuck up and I ain't gonna give him that satisfaction," Keon said, grabbing the can of Red Bull from Lavender. "You gonna grab the door?"

"Yeah, in a minute," Lavender said, leaning over the counter in a way that allowed Keon to see down her low-cut sweater. "I need to talk to you about your schedule," Lavender started. The constant noise from the bell was starting to drive her insane. "Hold that thought." Lavender rushed over to the door and opened it. She stood there with her hand on her hip and stared Toni down. A mink stole covered her shoulders and arms and she wore a matching fur hat. She wore a pair of cream-colored tights and Burberry checked rain boots. A mono-grammed Louis Vuitton bag graced her arms and a pair of Dior shades covered her eyes.

"Hello, Lavender," Toni said, moving to side so she could get by and enter the club.

Lavender blocked her and gave her a fake smile. "Hello . . . What's your name again?" Lavender asked, continuing to block the door.

"My name is Toni," she said, clearing her throat. "Are you gonna let me in? It's cold out here."

"Sure, sure," Lavender said, finally stepping aside to allow her to enter the club.

Lavender watched closely as Toni walked past the bar and to the client lounge area. She and Keon locked eyes and quickly turned their heads. Lavender felt rage overcome her as she looked over at Keon who seemed to be fixated on the Red Bull can; it was clear that she had a thing for him. Lavender marched over the lounge area and stood in front of Toni, who was now talking on the phone.

"Excuse me, can I have a word with you?" Lavender asked, motioning for her to end her call.

Toni gave off a fake smile, nodded her head, motioned for her to give a minute, and continued talking.

Lavender leaned on one leg and tapped her foot. She could feel her body starting to warm up as she watched

Toni yap away on the phone for the next five minutes, ignoring her first attempt to get her off the phone. She couldn't wait to tell her that she was being banned from seeing Keon for the next two weeks.

"Is it time for my appointment?" Toni said, lowering her phone from her ear and placing it in her lap.

"As a matter of fact, it is. But before you go, I need to tell you that you're no longer scheduled to meet with Special K, you'll be meeting with King instead."

"What? Who is King?" Toni said, lowering herself back down in the recliner chair. "I made my appointment with Special K—I don't want to meet with King."

"Well, it's very obvious that you have a thing for Special K," Lavender said, making quotation marks in the air. "He's the only guy you have ever made appointments with here at the club. We like our members to have variety."

"What if I don't want variety?" Toni said, with her face all balled up.

"Well then you don't want to be a member of this club," Lavender shot back just as fast as the words rolled off of Toni's tongue.

"Fine," Toni said in a huff. "Can I please go back to my phone call?"

"Sure." Lavender smiled. "Whenever you're ready you can go on up."

Lavender turned around with a look of victory on her face and returned to the bar area. She noticed Keon turn around quickly when he noticed that she was coming back in his direction.

"K, I need to see you in my office," Lavender said, folding her arms in front of her. She sashayed up the steps and rounded the hallway. She continued down the long corridor until she reached her office and opened the door. She took a seat on the edge of her desk and waited for Keon to enter the room.

"Is something going on with you and Toni?" Lavender asked, staring into his eyes as if she could see straight through him.

"Naw, why you say that?" Keon asked, staring right back at her without so much as a blink.

"I see the way you look at her, Keon, I'm not stupid. I don't want to see you get yourself in trouble messing with a client," Lavender said. She wore a look of genuine concern on her face. "She's on a two-week hiatus from you."

"What?" Keon said, raising his voice. "Why? That's crazy."

"Because I see the writing on the wall, K. You got a thing for her and she damn sure has a thing for you. I'm hoping you're smart enough to stay away from her. So, during the hiatus, she can get to experience the other guys in the club, and hopefully it will calm down whatever this is she has going for you."

"I don't have a thing for her," Keon said, bringing his voice back down to its regular tone. "The only person I have a thing for is you." Keon pulled Lavender down on his lap. He held her face in his big, bear claw hands and kissed her sweetly on the lips.

She blushed. "You sure about that? Because if I find out you and that bitch Toni creepin' around outside the club, I'm going to cut your dick off and make you suck it."

"Damn, what type of shit is that?" Keon said, looking at her like she was crazy. "Is that what you told your ex-boyfriend?"

"No, I didn't tell my *ex-fiancé* that at all," Lavender said, kissing him on the lips again. "He was one of those niggas that thought he could get away with fuckin' me over. So I fucked him before he fucked me."

"So you cut his dick off?" Keon said, placing his hands around her waist and she straddled him.

"No, I killed him," Lavender said, unbuckling Keon's pants.

"You what?" Keon said, pulling her gray mohair sweater over her head.

"I killed him," Lavender said nonchalantly. "He cheated on me and I killed him."

"Are you serious?"

"Dead serious," Lavender said, unbuttoning his shirt. "But you don't have to worry about that, K, you know better than to cheat on me."

"Cheat on you . . . So, what, you sayin' we a couple?"

"What you think? You hit it raw, didn't you?" Lavender said, continuing to work on his shirt.

"Yeah, but . . ."

"Yeah, but nothing," Lavender said, opening the shirt, revealing a crisp white undershirt. "I don't care about you servicing these chicks in the club, but nobody else." Lavender kissed on his neck as she caressed his chest. She then got up from his lap, pulled his pants around his ankles along with his boxers, and accepted his swollen member in her hot, moist mouth.

"I . . . I don't know about that," Keon said, his voice trailing off as she pushed the tip of his dick so far in her mouth that it touched her tonsils.

"Hello," Lavender yelled into the phone over the car stereo as she made her way home from work.

"When you gonna have that money for me? The boss is getting impatient," Al said, coughing off of a stogie he just lit moments before.

Lavender swerved as she tried to lower the radio. "How much do I owe you?" Lavender asked, pulling over to the side of the road so she wouldn't get into an accident while she was talking on the phone.

"Eighteen grand," Al said. "And the boss wants his money no later than next week."

"I don't know if I can swing that by next week," Lavender huffed. "Can you talk to him and ask him to give me a little more time?"

"Sorry, hon. The boss ain't taking lightly to you owing him money again. He said if you don't have his money, he's going to come down and off you himself."

Lavender pressed the end button to her cell phone out of nervousness and threw it on the seat beside her. Her hands shook as she shifted the car out of park and into drive. She started off on the road again and the cell phone rang; it almost made her jump out of her skin. She peered over at the phone; it was Al calling her back. She tried her best to ignore the phone as she continued driving, but it was driving her mad. She grabbed it off the seat, rolled down the window, and threw the phone out.

Chapter 21

Lust, Love, and Lies
Keon

"Here I come," Keon yelled, making his way down the steps of his grandmother's quaint three-bedroom home.

The doorbell continued to ring out, echoing throughout the house. He couldn't understand for the life of him who the hell was leaning on the bell so damn hard. Luckily his grandmother was at a Bible retreat this weekend; otherwise, she would have called the cops before he could even get downstairs to answer. As he approached the front door, he looked over at the grandfather clock in the corner of the living room, which was illuminated by an oversized floor lamp with a pea green shade sitting beside it. The clock read well past one A.M. He stooped down to look through the peephole; it was Toni bobbing back in forth with her hands in her jacket pockets. He opened the door and stood in the doorway barechested, wearing a pair of red and white ball shorts and some white ankle socks.

"What are you doing here?" Keon said, yawning while holding the door open. "It's late as shit."

"I want you so fuckin' bad right now," Toni said, bursting through the front door and grabbing Keon's face in her hands.

She pressed her lips against his so hard and so long that his dick got rock hard in a matter of five seconds. He pulled her close and closed the door behind him all without coming up for air. He ran his hands through her thick, dark brown, shoulder-length mane, and pinned her against the door with his large, muscular frame.

"Tell daddy what you want," Keon said, grinding up against her.

"I want some of that big, juicy dick of yours," Toni whined, reaching in his pants and swirling her finger around the tip of his head.

"Come on upstairs and let daddy wear that ass out," he said, smacking her on the ass.

"Can we do it with the lights on?" she asked, biting her bottom lip like a little girl. She looked at him as if he were a steak dinner, ready to eat him whole while continuing to stroke his swollen member.

"Whatever you want," he replied, stepping aside and letting her lead the way to his bedroom.

Keon stood in the doorway of his small rectangular-shaped bedroom and watched as Toni stripped down to a lacey purple bra and panty set. He grasped his still hardened dick and stroked it as she undid her bra and threw it at him. She stepped out of her panties and threw them at him as well. He picked them up from his feet and smelled the crotch like an animal scouting its prey.

He looked into her eyes; they sparkled like two little round emeralds.

"I'm outta condoms," Keon said, sifting through his dresser drawers like a madman. "I'ma have to run to the 7-Eleven and grab some." Keon slammed the dresser drawer closed and grabbed his Nike sweat-pants from the floor. He then slid on his shower shoes and grabbed his matching track jacket from the chair.

"No, no, no, don't do that," Toni said, sitting on the side of the bed naked with her legs crossed Indian style. "I should have a box in the console of the car."

"I'll be right back," Keon said, licking his lips while peering in between her thighs. "Don't start without me."

As Keon approached Toni's silver-colored Mercedes with the key in hand, the doors automatically unlocked. He slid into the driver's seat and closed the door. He opened the console and sifted around for the condoms she said she had stashed inside. After digging through a pile of crumbled-up receipts and candy wrappers, it was clear to Keon that there were no signs of condoms anywhere in the consol. *Maybe she meant the glove compartment,* he thought as he grabbed the handle to open it. He reached in without looking and ran his hand across a cold metal object. Keon instantly became startled and snatched his hand away, causing the remnants of the compartment to fall on the floor in a loud thump.

Keon turned on the dome light in the car and his jaw dropped open; there on the floor lay a Glock handgun in a heap of papers. Keon bent over the seat and started picking up the papers that fell out, leaving the gun as the last item that needed to be put back in its proper place. As he got to the last few pieces of paper, he noticed a leather wallet lying over to the side by the door. He reached over as far as he could and used the tips of his fingers to push it over closer in his direction, causing it to flip open. There was a driver's license and a metal badge sitting side by side. Keon picked it up and held it close to his face; there was a picture of a fat chick by the name of Maria Ortiz. He looked over the details; they all matched Toni's height and eye color. He didn't notice the address, though; it seemed to be not far from where he lived. Keon continued surveying the wallet; the metal badge was that of the Philadelphia Police Department. He sat back in the driver's seat and looked at the driver's license photo again, but this time much closer than before. Keon felt as though his mind was playing tricks on him; it looked like Toni for sure. He looked at the date that the photo was taken; it was due to expire in about two months.

Keon hurried and stuffed everything back in the glove compartment and closed it. He sat up in the driver's seat, frozen solid. He didn't know whether to confront her or ignore it. He knew one thing: he had to tell Lavender everything. Keon's thoughts were interrupted by Toni, who was now knocking on the window, motioning for him to open the door.

"Well?" she said, rubbing her arms from the frigid cold.

"Well what?" Keon asked, looking at her like she was a complete stranger.

"Did you find the condoms?"

"Oh yeah, the condoms . . . Naw, ain't none," he said, snapping back to reality. "I gotta go to the store to grab some." Keon got out of the car and started up the street. He needed time to think anyway. He had to figure out how he was going to get out of the situation without looking suspicious.

"K, wait a minute," Toni said, heading in his direction. "We don't need any condoms, just pull out." She grabbed his arm and led him back to the house.

"I . . . I . . . I don't feel comfortable doin' that," Keon said, following her by the hand.

"It'll be fine, just trust me," she said, pulling him in the front door and closing it behind him.

***

For the next month, Keon canceled every session with Toni on the books. He either called out on the days that she scheduled or left before it was time for her arrive. He found himself spending more and more time with Lavender, staying at her crib with her, dicking her head off night after night. It was the only way he was able to keep his mind off Toni and the situation at hand. Lavender never questioned him about it; in fact, she enjoyed the time he was spending with her. The only problem was that Keon was starting to lose money. With him dodging Toni, it was hard for him to service his other clients as he did before. He was too paranoid that the place was going to get raided. He had to talk to someone; otherwise, he was going to go crazy.

It was a Sunday afternoon and the club was bare. One client sat in the lounge area waiting to be serviced and two others sat in the corner of the bar drinking and chatting amongst themselves. Keon sat toward the middle of the bar, spaced out.

"I fucked up," Keon admitted, chugging down a vodka and tonic.

He slammed the glass down on the bar and waited patiently for Rafiq to pour him another. He rubbed his hands through his hair and let out a long sigh.

"What you mean, you fucked up?" Rafiq asked, placing another glass in front of him.

Keon motioned for Rafiq to move in closer and then said, "That broad Toni is a fuckin' cop, man."

"What?" Rafiq shouted, causing the two patrons in the corner to turn in their direction.

"Keep your voice down—damn," Keon said, smiling to acknowledge the customers who were gawking at them in hopes that they would return to their own individual conversations.

"You better go tell Lav so she can take care of it," Rafiq said, dumping a dishpan of glasses in the sink to be washed.

"It's not that easy," Keon said, downing the glass of vodka that was in front of him. "I told her everything."

"Everything—like what?" Rafiq asked, pouring Keon yet another drink.

"We been fuckin' around for a few months now—outside the club," Keon whispered, avoiding direct eye contact with Rafiq.

Rafiq lost the grip on the glass that he was about to place in the rack above the bar and it came crashing down on the floor, scattering little shards of glass everywhere. He quickly grabbed the broom out of the corner by the register area and started sweeping it up.

"So what you gonna do?" Rafiq asked, picking up the glass with a dustpan.

"I'ma just go tell Lavender what happened—what else can I can do?" Keon said, finishing off the last of his drink and wiping his mouth with his sleeve.

Rafiq stopped dead in his tracks and gave Keon a blank stare. "Are you fuckin' crazy? If she finds out you was dating that bitch outside the club your ass gonna wind up in a fuckin' body bag quicker that you can spell your own name. I told you not to fuck around. You dumb-ass niggas never listen. Y'all wanna be all curious and shit. Don't you know curiosity killed the cat? Damn!" Rafiq shook his head at Keon and continued cleaning up at the bar. "Remember the dude I told you about when you first started here? You know, the one who infected the mayor's wife with HIV?"

Keon took a long pause as he recounted the conversation which took place several months ago and then said, "Yeah, I remember that. What about him?"

"It was always said that she sent him away, like, out of town. Well, that's what she told the boys at least.

Anyway, that nigga got rocked when he got in the cab to go to the airport. They found his body slumped over in the back seat with two to the forehead."

"So what the fuck am I supposed to do?" Keon asked, leaning over the bar, making sure no one else was listening to their conversation. "Tell me what to do," Keon pleaded.

"Get rid of the bitch," Rafiq said, staring into Keon's eyes. "Need I say more?"

Keon leaned back off the bar and sat back down. He understood perfectly what Rafiq meant.

"I . . . I . . . I can't do that, man," Keon stuttered. "I'm no fuckin' killa."

"You bitchin' up now? You shoulda thought about that shit before you took that broad personal," Rafiq said, wiping down the surface of the bar.

"I ain't no bitch," Keon said, deepening his tone. "I just ain't *that* type of dude."

"It's either kill or be killed, playboy—the choice is yours," Rafiq said, casually looking up here and there at Keon while he continued handling his business.

"Listen, man, I need your help," Keon said, sounding like a lost puppy. "I'm all over the place, man. I don't want go back to jail."

Rafiq threw the dishtowel in the sink and came around the bar to join Keon on the stool beside him. He folded his hands on the bar with his index fingers pointed upward.

"Are you gonna help me or what?" Keon blurted out, turning in Rafiq's direction. "I've been avoiding her because I didn't know what else to do."

"Call her up and tell her to meet you here at the club tonight after close and I'll take care of the rest," Rafiq said, reaching behind the bar to grab a cigar. He clipped the tip off, lit it, and took several short puffs.

"What are you going to do to her?"

"Does it really matter?" Rafiq asked, giving off a confused look. "Just make sure you have her here and in your room by the time the club closes."

"A'ight, a'ight, I got you," Keon said, getting up from his seat. "I'ma go get dressed and get outta here. I'm done for the day."

Rafiq looked over at the clock; it was a little after 7:00 P.M. and he was due to leave once Lavender arrived to take over. "See you lata," Rafiq said, flicking ashes into the ashtray in front of him.

Chapter 22

Murder with a Deadly Weapon
Rafiq

"I gotta go handle some business," Rafiq said, putting his coat back on just a few hours after he'd taken it off. "Don't wait up." He kissed his wife on the cheek and headed back out the door. Rafiq just came home to check the house and see what she and the kids were up to; otherwise, he would have just stayed at work. After catching her cheating, he made sure that he kept his eye on Farrah. So if that meant wasting time and gas just to pop in and out, that's exactly what he did.

As Rafiq pulled out of the driveway, all he could think about was how foolish Keon was. He knew he was going to get wrapped up in one of the clients; he could sense it the day Lavender hired him. Usually in a situation like this, he would have gone straight to Lavender and had her handle it, but this time was different. He had to help Keon in order to help himself.

Rafiq rolled up a blunt and took a few puffs as he paced back in forth in front of the building. He closed his eyes and exhaled the smoke through his nose. Rafiq hadn't smoked in a while but since he was having problems at home, it was the only thing that soothed him. He looked down at his watch; it was one A.M. By now, Keon and Toni should be inside, and he should be able to get in and get the job done and get out. Rafiq finished his blunt and threw the stump to the ground. He pulled a leather glove out of each of his jacket pockets. He placed them on his hands and opened the door to the club with his key. He hurried inside and headed toward the safe to grab the spare key to Lavender's room, where the surveillance camera monitors were located. He clicked the switch to the off position and the screens instantly became blank. He locked the office back up and headed down the hallway toward Keon's room.

He placed his ear to the door; he could hear Toni moaning as if they were having sex. He sat and listened for a moment, waiting for the perfect moment to bust in and make his move. Rafiq clasped his gloves together, making sure they fitted as he needed them to. Rafiq opened the door and eased in; it was pitch-black inside. He felt his way around the room until he reached the bed.

"Oh my God, I think someone is in here," Toni yelled, jumping up and running smack-dab into Rafiq.

He felt her hair brush his shoulder and grabbed a fistful of it and threw her to the floor.

"Get off of me," Toni yelled, kicking Rafiq in the chin.

"You fuckin' bitch," he yelled, feeling around in the dark for her face. He could feel the blood starting to ooze from his lip. "K, cut the fuckin' light on."

Keon hurried over to the wall and flicked the light switch on. He then moved to a nearby corner, where he wouldn't be in the way.

When the lights turned on, Rafiq grabbed her by the neck and threw her against the wall; he didn't expect her to fight back. He punched her in the face and she returned with a jab to his. Rafiq's body grew hot as he became more and more infuriated that he actually had to put in work. He grabbed her by the hair once more and ran her into the wall again, this time face first. When he turned her back around, her nose and mouth were both bloody.

"Get off of me," Toni yelled again, grabbing at Rafiq's face. She was unable to reach it because of how he was holding her. "Keon, please . . . help me. . . ."

"Yeah, Keon, help her." Rafiq chuckled, grabbing her by the neck and squeezing it tightly.

"Keon, please," Toni said through short breaths. "Don't let him do this to me."

Keon stood in the corner, frozen still, unable to process what was going on; he felt like he was in a low-budget horror flick.

"Hand me that pillowcase," Rafiq said, continuing to squeeze her neck. "I'm tired of looking at this bitch face."

Keon snapped out of his trance and grabbed a pillow from the bed. He dumped the pillow out and handed Rafiq the pillowcase as instructed, all while continuing to stare at Toni, whose eyes were bulging out of her head from the lack of oxygen.

"Fuck," Rafiq yelled, as he took a blow to his shin as Toni made her last attempt to get away. "You dumb bitch," Rafiq said, dropping the pillowcase to the floor and punching her in the eye. "Get the pillowcase for me," Rafiq said, continuing to squeeze what little life was left from Toni's petite frame.

Keon reached over the side of the bed and grabbed the pillowcase and handed it to Rafiq. He looked at Toni one last time; her eyes kept opening and closing as she slipped in and out of consciousness.

Rafiq placed the pillowcase over her head and squeezed as tight as he could with both hands until her body fell limp. Once she stopped moving, he lowered her to the ground and removed the pillowcase.

"Damn, that bitch like a fuckin' superhero or something . . . She just wouldn't die," Rafiq joked, looking over at Keon, who was back over near the corner. "What the fuck are you doing over there all huddled up like a punk bitch? Shit, you should have been over here helping me take this broad out. I'm over here cleaning up your mess and your ass just watchin'. That's okay. You can bury the bitch 'cause I ain't gonna do that part for you."

Just as Rafiq was walking off, Toni started to cough. He rushed back over to her, punched her in the other eye, and grabbed the pillowcase and wrapped it around her neck. He pulled tighter and tighter until a red line was embedded in her skin.

"I told you that bitch was a superhero." Rafiq laughed, walking off once more, but this time sure that she was indeed taken care of.

"So what we gonna do wit' the body?" Keon said, peering over the edge of the bed at Toni's lifeless, abused corpse.

"Nigga, were you not just here when I said you were going to bury it?" Rafiq said, looking over at him and then at the large Persian rug that covered the floor in his room. "Help me move the bed so we can use the rug to wrap her up in." Rafiq grabbed one side of the bed and Keon the other and they pushed it aside. "Run downstairs and grab that roll of duct tape that's under the bar counter."

Keon nodded and made his way downstairs and back upstairs within a matter of a minute. He handed the roll of tape to Rafiq and waited for his next set of instructions.

"Roll her over on the carpet," Rafiq instructed, pulling a long piece of tape away from the roll.

Keon hesitated as he stood over Toni's limp body. He turned his head sideways and fought back tears. "I can't do it," he said, backing away from the body.

"Aww, nigga, I know you ain't about to cry on me," Rafiq said in his little baby voice.

"Fuck you, man," Keon said, bursting into tears.

"Get yaself together. Damn, you the one fucked up. You gotta eat this shit and do what you gotta do," Rafiq said, rolling her body over to the carpet with his foot. "Now, I got her on the carpet . . . You roll it up while I tape."

Keon wiped at his nose and bent over to start rolling the carpet. He stopped once her body was fully covered so Rafiq could start taping it close. Once they were done, they moved the bed back in its place and left the carpet on the side where no one could see unless they entered the room all the way.

"So when we gonna bury her?" Keon asked, looking down at the rolled-up rug.

"Tomorrow night," Rafiq said, sitting on the side of the bed. He pulled an already rolled blunt from his jacket pocket as well as a lighter. He lit it and took a few short puffs. "Go to the U-Haul and rent a truck close to closing and meet me here in the parking lot around midnight."

"What am I supposed to do with the body until then?" Keon asked, glancing over at the bloodstains on the wall from Rafiq smashing her face in.

"Leave it right where it's at, housekeeping is off tomorrow so you don't have to worry about anyone coming in. Also, call out from work tomorrow. There's no way you can service clients with her lying beside the bed . . . Someone's bound to notice."

"A'ight then, I'ma get out of here," Keon said, pulling on his pants.

"Yeah, okay," Rafiq said, continuing to puff on the blunt, which was halfway gone. "You better clean up these walls before you go."

"And how the hell am I supposed to do that?" Keon asked, looking over at the stain again.

"A little bleach and water should do the trick," Rafiq said, finishing off the blunt.

"I don't even want to know why or how you know that," Keon said. "I'm going down to the janitor closet to get the bucket and some bleach."

"Nigga, I don't care what you do, I'm outta here," Rafiq said.

"You not gonna help me clean up?" Keon asked, looking confused.

"Heeelllll naw, I think I've done enough for the night. I'm going home to my wife and kids. See you tomorrow night ... and don't be late." Rafiq held the blunt between his lips as he got up from the bed and made his way out of the room and to the front door of the club. Once outside, he took one last toke from the blunt and threw it to the ground. Rafiq was finally satisfied. Keon was scared shitless and ready and willing to do whatever he told him to. Rafiq had him right where he wanted him: eating out of the palm of his hand.

Chapter 23

The Perfect Crime
December, 2008
Keon

Keon rubbed his chapped hands together and shoved them back in his jacket pockets. He scanned the park and noticed that even the animals that resided there seemed to be absent. The only noise that could be heard, for what seemed like miles, came from one lonely owl perched above the leafless tree where he and Rafiq had chosen to dump their package. The owl's large, translucent golden eyes peered through Keon's guilty soul and when it hooted, chills ran down Keon's spine.

He grabbed the shovel from the back of the U-Haul pickup truck he and Rafiq rented a few hours before. With only the faint glow from the truck's lights to guide him, Keon sighed as he thrust the shovel into the frozen December ground and lifted out the first bit of dirt. He knew this was a bad idea but, after all, he did break the rules. For as long as he had worked for Lavender, he'd never messed up like this. Falling for a client was out of the question but he just couldn't help himself; the sex they had went from being a cold fuck to warm, intimate lovemaking.

"Chill out, man," Rafiq said, leaning against the back of the U-Haul. "It'll be over before you know it and we can all go back to living our lives."

Rafiq studied the sweat beading on Keon's brow; he was definitely shaken. It didn't take much to talk Keon into doing a dirty deed. All he needed to do was remind him that he would end up back in the pen where he had already spent three years. No nigga wanted to go back after doing that kind of time, or *any* time to be exact.

Rafiq dug into the back pocket of his dark denim True Religion jeans and pulled out a blunt and a cigarette lighter. He ran his lips across the edge of the cigar paper as if he were sealing an envelope to make sure it was nice and tight. Rafiq then lit it up, allowing the smoke to fill the cool winter air. He took a few short drags and exhaled without the slightest sign of choking. He continued to toke on the blunt, watching as Keon shoveled away, not thinking once to step in and help him. Rafiq had taken care of the hard part—burying the body was the grunt work.

"Take a hit of this." Rafiq held the lit blunt out to Keon. "It'll calm you down."

Keon stared at the burning blunt, noting the weird smell emanating from it. He hesitated for a moment and then took the blunt from Rafiq's gloved hand. He held it in between his index finger and his thumb and laid his lips upon it as if he were kissing a virgin girl for the first time.

"What's in this shit?" he asked, instantly feeling lightheaded. His eyesight blurred and a harsh burning sensation built up in his throat. He squatted down to the ground in hopes of trying to gain back his senses, but lost his balance and landed on his ass. He coughed violently and beat on his chest, hoping to clear his lungs.

"Angel dust," Rafiq replied coldly. "Now either take another hit or pass me my shit back."

Keon held the blunt out to Rafiq, who grabbed it from his hand.

Rafiq immediately took another toke from the blunt and laughed. "Stop bitchin'. A little dust ain't never hurt nobody."

Rafiq closed his eyes as he inhaled. He'd smoked so much of it that, to him, it was like smoking a regular bag of weed. He held the blunt out to Keon, who was struggling to get up from the ground.

Without thinking twice, Keon seized the blunt and finished it off with three long drags. He threw the stump to the ground and took a deep breath, allowing the high to consume his body. If he was going to get through the night, he needed to be on. He snatched the shovel from the ground and continued digging, but this time choosing to pick up the pace.

Rafiq folded his arms and watched as Keon dug a hole like a man possessed. *That's it. Just keep doing what you doing,* Rafiq thought with a sly grin spread across lips.

After two long hours of digging, Keon finally finished, stopping briefly here and there to warm his hands. He tossed the shovel up from the hole and climbed out. It wasn't as deep as he would have liked it to be, but the bitter winter air was starting to get the best of him. Plus, he wanted to get home before anybody realized he was gone.

Keon half walked, half jogged over to the U-Haul, pulled open the back of the pickup truck, and began tugging at the rolled-up carpet, which had to weigh over 140 pounds. He lugged it off the truck and stopped to catch his breath.

"Can I get a little help?" Keon asked, dragging it toward the hole.

Rafiq clasped his hands together, making sure his gloves fit correctly, before grabbing one side of the carpet. Together, they hoisted it off the ground and rushed over to the freshly dug hole to drop it in. The carpet plunged to the bottom, landing with a loud thump.

Rafiq ran to the passenger side of the truck, then returned to Keon's side with a long metal flashlight that he pointed down the hole. The beam of light exposed that the duct tape, which had been wrapped around the carpet, had broken loose, revealing Toni's lifeless, bruised body. Her battered face was stained with red streaks, and two swollen eyes revealed the agony of her ordeal. Burgundy-colored dried blood lay caked around her once graceful neck and surrounded what had been a crisp white pillowcase used to take her last breaths.

Keon couldn't hold it in any longer. He stepped away from the hole and vomited what was left of the turkey and cheese hoagie he'd eaten for lunch. He wiped his mouth with the sleeve of his leather jacket, leaving fragments of his stomach contents on the cuff.

"Don't worry, my man, we did a good thing," Rafiq said, patting him on the shoulder in reassurance. "We would all be in jail if she would have given us up."

Rafiq switched the flashlight to his other hand, and held it steadily over the hole as Keon picked up his shovel.

As Keon collected himself and threw the first bit of dirt into the hole, he stared in shock as the dark bits and pieces of the earth covered Toni's distorted face. A tear swept down his left cheek as he prayed for God's forgiveness. Keon continued to cover Toni's body until it was complete buried. He smoothed it over; making sure it was nice and leveled and tossed the shovel to the ground to warm his hands which were so cold that he hardly had any feeling in them at all.

"Come on, we gotta get out of here," Rafiq said, motioning for Keon to follow him back to the truck. "I gotta take the truck back in a few hours and I wanna make sure it's clean when I do."

Keon nodded in agreement, picked the shovel up from the ground and tossed it over his shoulder. Once over at the truck, he placed it in the back and headed toward the passenger side. He grabbed the handle opened the door and slid in beside Rafiq. Keon looked over in the direction of the hole as Rafiq backed out of the grass and onto the main road. He remained silent, allowing his thoughts to get the best of him as they made their way through the city. Keon looked over at the clock on the dash of the truck as they pulled up the his house; it was well past four A.M.

Speckles of light from the morning sun seeped through the holey curtain in Keon's bedroom, awaking him from a deep sleep. He opened his eyes and let out a big yawn. His head pounded as if he'd been hit by a Mack truck, causing him to think about the events that happened only hours before. He'd spent most of the night lying in darkness, listening to his grandmother's plump Siamese cat, Rufus, crying in heat. Every time he closed his eyes he pictured Toni's lifeless body lying in the hole that he dug to bury her. His heart ached as he thought about not being able to hear her voice again. He reached under his mattress and pulled out a picture of her lying on his bed with a negligee on. Her hair covered the pillow and she was laughing at the funny faces he was making behind the camera. He wiped at the tears forming in his eyes and stuffed the photo back under his mattress. He looked over at the clock on the wall over his dresser; it was almost noon. He was due in at the club at one and he hadn't even budged.

Keon pried himself from the bed as if he were glued to it and headed toward the bathroom to take a shower. As he passed his grandmother's room, he noticed she was sitting in the rocking chair by her window with her crossword book lying in her lap. He crept in and placed her reading glasses on the bedside table along with the crossword book, and covered her with the throw that decorated the bottom of her bed. He then continued his way down the hall to the bathroom. Once inside, he turned on the spigot and then shower and waited for the water to heat up. Keon pulled the curtain back and got inside. The hot water beaded off his body, soothing his aching muscles. Keon held his head under the showerhead, wishing that some way he would drown. He didn't deserve to live after what he'd done. The guilt was eating at him so bad that he broke down and started crying like a little baby.

"You all right, son?" his grandmother said, cracking the bathroom door just enough to stick her head inside.

"Yeah, yeah, Big Ma, I'm cool," Keon said, wiping at his nose, and the water continued to fall on his naked body.

"Okay, now, I'll be downstairs if you need me," his grandmother said, closing the door and heading down the hallway.

Keon banged his fist on the tile in the shower and let out a loud wail. He slid down to the floor and just sat there. After twenty minutes, Keon finally reached over to turn the shower off and got out. As he dried off, he peeped at himself in the medicine cabinet mirror; his eyes were red and puffy and he looked pitiful. He knew that if he was going to pull this off he was going to have to get himself together. He wrapped the towel around his waist and hurried down the hallway to his room. Goose bumps penetrated his skin as the cool air hit him. Once in his room, Keon dropped Visine in his eyes to clear up the redness and started to get dressed.

His heart pounded as he opened the dresser drawer and a pair of Toni's Victoria's Secret boy shorts fell to the floor. He stuffed them back inside all the way down to the bottom of the drawer and continued getting dressed. He took a seat on the side of the bed and opened the bedside table, searching for his watch that he seemed to misplace, and came across the two-carat diamond ring he bought for Toni. He opened the box and stared at it; the brilliance of the diamond sparkled, leaving little rainbows on the bedroom wall. He quickly closed it and shut the drawer. He couldn't keep her off his mind, and although he didn't actually kill her, it was haunting his soul just the same.

Chapter 24

Let's Get Lifted
Lavender

Lavender sat on the toilet seat of the bathroom in her apartment with her knees tightly pressed together, and steadied her hand as she lifted a small amount of coke out of a plastic Baggie, on a nail file, toward her nose. She held her nostril and inhaled. She repeated the action twice more. She sat back and allowed the high to consume her. A trickle of blood crept down her nose and landed on her lip. She licked it off and closed her eyes. Lavender had been high nonstop for the past week and hadn't left the apartment in days. She'd been ignoring calls from everyone; she just wanted to keep to herself. She reeked of cheap liquor and cigarettes. Usually she never smoked cigarettes, but owing money to her dealer had her on edge. She managed to dodge him for over a month despite the fact that he had all of her car windows bashed in and her tires flattened. Although Lavender no longer had her cell phone, she was able to check her messages using a landline, and when she did it gave her nothing but more anxiety. After he taxed her for being late, she owed almost double what she did before, and no matter how she looked at it, she wasn't going to be able to swing it.

Usually in a situation like this she would handle the guy herself, but this was the Mob and she knew that she was way out of her league. Yes, she had contacts, but they knew her contacts and her contacts' contacts. She knew that she had to make a move. She could no longer afford to stay in Philadelphia; it just wasn't safe. Plus, word had gotten to her about one of their clients gone missing, and in Lavender's heart she knew that Keon most likely had something to do with it. It was only a matter of time before the club got raided, and Lavender couldn't wait around to see all of her hard work go down the drain. When the idea hit her, Lavender jumped up from the toilet seat and headed straight to her closet. She looked at the mounds of clothes she had inside and started picking selected pieces to get her through the rest of the winter. She was going to take a large overnight bag with her and flee the city. Lavender always wanted to move to Atlanta and this made perfect sense in her mind. She stuffed ten outfits and five pairs of shoes in a large Louis Vuitton carry-on bag. She figured she could buy undergarments when she got there. She threw her makeup bag in the mix and zipped the bag closed. She then got on the phone with an airline and booked a first-class flight on the first thing smoking to Atlanta, Georgia. Once her ticket was purchased, she called downstairs and had the front desk order her car service to take her past the club and then to the airport. They told her that it would arrive within an hour's time.

Lavender hurried over to the kitchen and opened the cabinet under the sink and returned with a large Ziploc Freezer Bag full of hundred dollar bills. She opened it up and counted it; there was $6,000 total. She placed it back in the bag and stuffed it in her purse. She knew the safe at the club had at least ten grand in it. That would be enough for her to start over. She rushed through her condo, looking room to room, making sure she didn't leave anything of importance. With her purse on her arm and her carry-on bag on her shoulder, Lavender went out the door. She got all the way to the elevator and had to double back; she left the Baggie full of coke on the bathroom sink. Once she retrieved it she made her way down to the lobby. The car service she requested was standing by. The cold winter air whipped Lavender in the face as she handed the driver her bag and waited for him to open the door for her. She slid in the back seat and gave him the directions to the club. With the night sky and the tinted windows, Lavender was unable to see if anyone was following them. She rocked back and forth, impatiently waiting for them to arrive at her destination. The parking lot was vacant when she pulled up.

"Wait for me here," Lavender said, opening the car door. She hustled through the parking lot and opened the door with her key.

She locked the door behind her and headed behind the bar to the safe. She bent down, pressed in the code, and it beeped twice to let her know it was open. She pulled out four large stacks of money; there was twenty grand inside, way more than she anticipated. Excitement filled her as she thought about ditching her debt and everything else to start anew. She stuffed the money in her purse and grabbed a pen and pad from beside the cash register. She scribbled a note for Rafiq, placed it in the empty safe and closed it back up. When she stood back up, Keon was right behind her.

Lavender almost jumped out of her skin. "Damn, K, why the hell you sneakin' up on me like that?"

"My bad, I ain't mean to scare you," Keon said, throwing his hands up. "I was upstairs in my room and I heard a noise so I came down."

"What you doin' here anyway?" Lavender said, looking at him in a suspicious manner. "Word is that chick Toni is missing . . . Do you know anything about that?"

"Naw, I ain't hear nothing like that," Keon said, clearing his throat. "Maybe she went on vacation or something. What you doing here this time of night anyway?" Keon asked, changing the subject. He moved in closer to Lavender, studying her still glassy eyes.

"Oh, I had to grab some paperwork to catch up on," Lavender blurted out, pursing her lips. "I was sick . . . I had the flu," Lavender said, giving off a fake cough that even she herself didn't believe.

"So where you on your way to now?" Keon asked, peering down at his watch. "It's one A.M."

"I know what time it is," Lavender said, cursing herself for taking so much time up at the club. She was supposed to be in and out within minutes. Her flight was scheduled to leave at 5:00 A.M., and even though she would be early she wanted to get to the airport safe and sound. Once in the airport Al and the boys couldn't really do too much to harm her. "I'm on my way back home now," Lavender lied, backing up and then turning toward the door.

"You feel like some company?" Keon asked, starting behind her.

"*No.*" Lavender's voice rose. "I mean, no. I'm still sick," she said, coughing again. "I'll hit you up tomorrow to let you know how I'm feeling, then you can come over then. Oh yeah, tell Rafiq it's a note for him in the safe." Lavender started toward the door again. She left and made her way back to the tinted-up Lincoln. When she got inside, she ordered the driver to take her to the airport.

Twenty minutes later, the car pulled up in front of the entrance to the airport. Lavender got out of the car and waited for the driver to place her bag on the sidewalk. She gave him a generous tip and went in. Once inside, a feeling of relief swept over Lavender's body.

There was enough security around that there was no way that Al could do anything to her. She wheeled her bag over to the ticket counter and gave them her ID and credit card. They processed her ticket immediately and she was off to the security checkpoint.

Once in line, Lavender remembered she had that Baggie of coke in her purse. She jumped out of line as quickly as she got in it. With her ticket under her arm, she grabbed her carry-on and headed toward the bathroom to dump the bag. Lavender opened the door to the bathroom and went straight to the handicapped stall. She locked the door and dumped her bag on the floor. She rustled around in her purse until she came to the bag, which was about halfway full. She opened it up and held it over the toilet. *It would be stupid to dump it,* Lavender thought. *I might as well get high before I get on the plane.* Lavender backed away from the toilet and grabbed a seat cover from the wall by the sink. She placed it on the toilet seat and sat on it. She rummaged through her purse once more to find her square-shaped compact mirror and a twenty dollar bill. Lavender held the mirror on her lap and folded the twenty in half to use it to scoop the coke out of the bag. She then separated it into four lines, rolled the twenty up, and held it and the mirror up toward her nose.

She dragged the twenty the length of each line as she inhaled them like a vacuum cleaner. Once the four lines were done she scooped some more, repeating the same actions as before until the entire bag was empty. Lavender's heart was beating out of her chest. Her body was so hot that she felt like she was in a sauna. Lavender jumped up from the toilet seat and rushed over to the sink. She turned on the cold water and splashed it in her face in hopes of cooling herself off. Her heart continued to race and pains shot through her chest as she leaned

on the sink and looked in the mirror at her reflection;
her eyes were bloodshot and she was starting to panic.
The pains in her chest increased. Lavender could feel
her body give way and fall to the ground. Her body
jerked violently in wild spasms for several minutes and
then finally fell still. Her heart gave out three last pumps
and abruptly stopped beating. She lay on the floor, un-
conscious, until she completely slipped away.

Chapter 25

Trust No Man
Keon

Keon crept into his grandmother's bedroom and removed her reading glasses from her face with ease. He placed them and the Bible that was lying on her chest on the bedside table and turned off the lamp. He closed the door behind him and started down the steps. The phone started to ring, causing him to run down them and answer it; he didn't want it to wake his grandmother up. If it did, there would be hell to pay.

"Hello," Keon said, panting from the sprint from the stairwell.

"Hey, man, what's up?" Marquise whispered, hoping Keon wouldn't hang up.

"Marquise? Is that you?" Keon asked, opening the fridge and taking a container of orange juice from the top shelf. He unscrewed the top and took a long swig from the carton. Keon hadn't seen or heard from Marquise in months. The last time they spoke was when they had the big argument about leaving Lavender alone. Keon couldn't take Marquise's jealous behavior; it caused him to back away. He still put money on his books and made sure he was taken care of, but he did it in silence.

"Yeah, man, it's me. I need to talk to you about something."

"Well, you got me. What's going on?" Keon asked.

Marquise rocked back and forth as he held the receiver in his hand, trying to find the right words to say. "I'm sorry, man," Marquise said, looking at the dialing pad on the pay phone as if it were Keon's face. Water formed in the corner of his eyes. "I had no choice but to tell them about the club."

"You did what?" Keon said, choking on his last gulp of orange juice. "Who did you tell about the club, man? What the hell you talking about?"

"I copped a deal with the DA. They knew I knew about Lavender and her operation and they wanted info. They offered me a deal I couldn't refuse—I had to take it, otherwise, I would have rotted in this muthafucka. I didn't think that it would affect you, man . . . They promised me you wouldn't have anything to worry about. They just wanted her but the undercover they sent in is missing and they think you have something to do with it because she was pregnant with your baby."

"Pregnant? Are you serious, Marquise?" Keon asked, leaning against the kitchen wall. "Who told you she was pregnant?"

"Listen, the DA told me that she was . . . They was just about to pull her from the job . . . They found out that she actually fell for you and they had to pull her. The DA wanted me to rat on you . . . They think you did something to her. . . ." Marquise said, lowering his voice. "They coming for you, man. You gotta get outta there."

"Where the hell am I going to go?" Keon asked, leaving the kitchen and entering the dining room. He continued traveling toward the front of the house to peek out the window. He lifted the shade up; there was no one there. "What did you tell them, Marquise?"

"I didn't tell them nothing. I told them that you and I ain't spoke in months and that I had no idea where you were. I'm pretty sure after this conversation they'll know I've spoke to you but that's it," Marquise said, looking over at the guard who was quickly approaching while he continued his conversation. "I don't know where to tell you to go . . . Just get outta town. I don't even want to know what happened to her or if you had anything to do with it. I'm asking you as your friend, your best friend . . . Please, Keon, just pack a bag and roll, man."

Before Keon could respond, the phone went dead. He hung up and hurried upstairs to pack a bag as Marquise had instructed. He moved the bed, which sat on the side of the wall, and bent down by the mattress. He found the small slit he made to keep his stash and forced his oversized hands inside, grabbing as many bills as possible. Keon stuffed them in his duffel bag along with the a few pairs of boxer briefs, two pairs of jeans, and several thermal shirts. He leaned on the bag and zipped it closed. He threw it on his shoulder and headed downstairs. He thought about calling to warn Lavender, but he'd been calling her for days and she hadn't responded. Before he could leave, the phone rang again; he was hoping it was Marquise.

"Hello," Keon answered, pacing back and forth in the kitchen.

"Yo, man, it's Rafiq."

"Hey, what's going on?" Keon asked, placing his one free hand in his pocket.

"Lavender called me and said the cops came there looking for us." Rafiq's voice trembled. "I need you to meet me at my crib so we can get out of town, man. I got somewhere for us to go."

"A'ight, a'ight, I be there in like an hour," Keon said, looking at the clock on the wall. "I'm gonna have to go to the ave and catch a hack up there."

"Come through the back way. I see you when you get here," Rafiq said, hanging the phone up.

Keon placed the phone on the hook and grabbed his leather jacket from the coat rack. He turned off all the lights downstairs, leaving him to maneuver in complete darkness. Keon felt his way around until he reached the front door. He peeked out the living room window; there was still no one around. He left the house with nothing but the clothes on his back and the small duffel bag on his shoulder. He slid his keys in the mailbox; from the looks of things, he wouldn't need them anymore. He looked into the night sky; snow flurries fell, covering the bare tree branches. Cars were almost completely covered, and so was the pavement.

As Keon tracked his way through the snow to the avenue to catch a hack, he couldn't help but to think about Toni and their unborn child. He cursed himself for listening to Rafiq. He should have just told Lavender what was going on and suffered whatever consequences that came down the pike. He would have rather put himself on the line than her and their child. Keon fought back tears as the winter wind cut his face like a dull blade. He placed his hands in his jacket pockets and continued trudging through the snow, which was starting to fall even heavier now. When he reached the avenue, he propositioned the first hack man he saw with a fee of one hundred dollars and he was off to Bensalem to meet Rafiq at his house.

When Keon arrived at Rafiq's house, all of the lights were off except for the floodlight that lit up the driveway. Keon walked up the small path opposite the driveway in pure darkness with only the faint light of the street lamp to guide him until he reached the back door. He lifted his arms to knock and then hesitated; for some reason he didn't feel comfortable. For some reason, Keon couldn't help to wonder why Lavender would have called Rafiq to warn him about the cops coming to the club and not him. Keon knocked lightly at the door; it opened right after. Keon peered into the darkened house; he couldn't see a thing. He stepped inside and closed the door behind him. He could hear several footsteps and then the light over the kitchen stove popped on.

"Hey, K, how you doin'?" Farrah said, forcing a smile across her face. She wore a pair of fuzzy slide-on slippers and a yellow plush bathrobe that fell to her ankles. Her hair was pulled up in a tight bun. Red lipstick was slathered across her lips and mascara lined her eyes.

"Hey, Farrah, I'm cool. Where's Rafiq?" Keon asked, looking around the kitchen as if he was going to pop up at any minute now.

"He stepped out for a minute to grab a few dollars from the ATM machine. He told me to have you wait for him upstairs in the den. "

Keon nodded and headed across the kitchen toward the stairwell. He climbed the steps and entered the den area with Farrah following right behind him. He dropped his duffel bag and took a seat on the leather couch by the window. Keon unzipped his coat and made himself comfortable. He closed his eyes in hopes of catching a catnap. Keon could feel Toni's petite hands rubbing his shoulders and her soft kisses graze his neck and across his cheek until they reached his lips. Keon's dream was starting to feel too real. He forced his eyes open and, to his surprise, Farrah was straddled on top of him with nothing on. Her bathrobe was on the floor, as was her bra and panty set.

"What are you doing?" Keon said, pushing her off of him. He touched his lips and looked at his fingers; her red lipstick stained them.

"There he is, Officer," Rafiq said, pointing at Keon on the couch.

"Rafiq? What the fuck, man? You just gonna turn me in? What about you, man? You killed her . . . and the other dude."

"Keon, why don't you stop it. The police already know you killed both Edward and Toni. I told them the truth already: you and Farrah was having an affair for over a year now. They know you threatened to kill me if I told anyone about what happened."

Keon looked at Farrah; her eyes were glued to the floor. "Farrah, tell them the truth. Tell them that Rafiq killed that guy, not me. Tell them," Keon yelled at the top of his lungs.

"He's right, we've been sleeping around for a year now. He caught me with Edward and snapped. He told me himself that he killed Edward and buried him in the park. He threatened Rafiq and told him he would kill him and my kids if he ever said a word," Farrah said, unable to look Keon in the eye.

"Farrah, are you fuckin' kidding me?" Keon yelled. "She's lying! They're both lying! Please! You gotta believe me . . . I didn't hurt either one of them."

"Cuff 'im," the detective said, walking over to Keon and grabbing the duffel bag from beside him. He unzipped and dumped it, and rummaged through it. "Sure looks like you were trying to get out of town to me. Huh, you guys are all the same. You think you can get away with anything you want, but not today, homeboy. If I have anything to do with it, you'll never be a free man again . . . in life."

"He's lying," Keon said again, this time in a much defeated tone. Keon got up from the couch and held his hands behind his back and waited for the officer to place the cuffs on his wrists. It was a routine that he was all too familiar with.

"And take these two down to the station for questioning," the detective said, looking over at Rafiq, whose slick smile turned into a look of concern.

"Why we gotta go down to the station?" Rafiq asked, looking quite confused. "I gave y'all what y'all wanted. I turned in the killer."

"Sure you did, son, now you shouldn't mind answering some questions. Don't worry, we won't keep you long. You and the missus here should be out and on your way home before daybreak," the detective said, looking over at Farrah, who was balled up by the couch with her robe covering her naked body.

Keon stared at Rafiq as they ushered him away in handcuffs; he shook his head as their eyes met. He ought to have known better than to trust Rafiq. Keon's mind was racing; Rafiq had set him up. He thought back to Rafiq's actions when they were burying the body. The leather gloves he wore, him insisting that Keon bury the body alone. Why didn't he see the signs? It was too late; no one believed him and he was going to spend the rest of his life in the pen. The woman he loved was dead, as was his unborn child, all because of him. Keon couldn't trust anyone anymore; they were all too busy praying for his downfall.

When Keon arrived at the station, there was already a wagon there waiting to transport him back to prison. They processed the paperwork and within forty-five minutes he was on the road headed toward Graterford Prison. By the time he reached his destination, it was daybreak. The guards unloaded Keon and two others, and lead them toward the inside for processing.

As he passed through the security checkpoints, Keon came across a familiar face: it was the same guard who let him out a year ago. The guard looked him over and took a bite from his cream-filled donut as he signed the intake paperwork. "I knew you'd be back. Y'all all come back," he said, pressing the buzzer and opening the gate to the cell block.

Keon climbed up on the top bunk and propped his arms behind his head. He stared up at the ceiling and all he could think about is how he failed not only himself but his daughter. He knew his grandmother would be disappointed in him; she was the only one that had faith him in and he let her down as well. Toni was dead and so was their unborn child. He no longer deserved to live, knowing the pain he caused others because of his stupid decisions. With tears in his eyes, he removed the sheet off his bed and prepared to take his own life.

Chapter 26

The Ultimate Betrayal
Rafiq

Rafiq dialed Lavender's cell phone for the twentieth time and it went straight to voice mail. He decided that he was going to go past her apartment building today and use the spare key to see what the hell was going on. He'd left her a voice mail to warn her about the situation with Keon and also to tell her that he was going to shut the club down until things cooled off. In his mind, Lavender was probably somewhere all high and coked up; that was the only time when she ignored his calls.

Rafiq unlocked the door to the club and went inside. It had been a week to date since Keon had gotten locked up, and since then the club had been closed down. He wanted to go past there a long time ago but, with all the questioning from the police, it just didn't seem safe. Now that things had died down some, Rafiq decided that he was going to go inside, grab whatever he could of value, and roll. He already knew the club wouldn't be reopening. Not only did he turn Keon in, he also dropped the dime on Lavender. He had the DA eating out of his hand; all he had to do was testify against the two of them and they would let him walk away scot-free. They were going to look the other way when it came to his involvement with the club and place him and his family in the Witness Protection Program. He was looking forward to starting over with his wife and family. They already had a house in upstate New York picked out and most of their belongings had been shipped there.

Rafiq locked the door and opened the swinging door to the bar. He figured he would hit the safe first, as it should have been fully loaded because none of the boys had gotten paid their last week of wages before the club actually shut down. He bent down and pressed the code in; it beeped two times to alert him that it was unlocked. He opened it up and felt around; it was empty except for a small sheet of loose leaf paper. He grabbed it and looked it over. His skin turned red and beads of sweat formed on his brow. He balled the piece of paper up and threw it across the room.

"Fuckin' bitch," Rafiq yelled out, causing his words to echo through the club.

Lavender had taken all the money from the safe and run off. Rafiq cursed to himself. His deal was to turn in Keon and Lavender, and with her leaving town, he wasn't sure if his deal would be so sweet. He continued traveling through the club, entering and searching every room, looking for anything that was worth some dough. He found a few hundred dollars here and there and placed them in his back pocket. The last room he went in was Keon's. He turned the room inside out, looking for whatever he could find. He sat down on the side of the bed and opened the nightstand drawer. He pulled out a little satin box and opened it up; there was a two-carat, princess-cut diamond inside, sparkling so bright that he almost needed sunglasses to look at it. He placed the ring on his pinky finger and chucked the box on the bed.

As Rafiq left the club, all he could think about was what he could do to ensure that his deal still went through. Finally an idea hit him: he would turn in all the clients as well as the employees. That would keep him out of trouble for sure. He doubled back around the block and went back inside to grab all of the records from Lavender's office. He whistled as he carried them under his arm and out the door. He got back in the car, placed the files on the back seat, and drove off. His phone rang as he merged onto the expressway heading home. He looked down at the caller ID; it was Farrah.

"Hey, baby, what time you coming home?" Farrah asked.

Rafiq hadn't gotten a call from her like this in a long time. Ever since he caught her wrong she sort of stayed to herself. *She is finally coming around and trying to make things work,* Rafiq thought.

"Hey, baby, I'm on my way now," Rafiq said, changing lanes. "I'll be home shortly."

"See you when you get here," Farrah said, hanging the phone up.

Rafiq pressed the end button and threw his phone on the seat beside him. He pressed the play button on the CD player and zoned out. Maxwell's "Ascension (Don't Ever Wonder)" blared from the speakers. It was a good day in Rafiq's book. No, he didn't get the money, but he damn sure got the girl. His wife was acting like her usual self again and he loved it. He looked at his pinky finger in front of him on the steering wheel; he was going to give that ring to Farrah. She was going to go nuts when she saw it.

When Rafiq pulled up in the driveway, all the lights to the house were off, even the outside floodlights. He turned the car off and got out. He traveled up the darkened walkway until he reached the side door to the kitchen. He opened the door and flicked on the light above the stove.

"Farrah," Rafiq called out.

"I'm in the family room, baby," Farrah answered.

"What you doing?" Rafiq asked, traveling through the kitchen to the family room. He opened the kitchen door that led to the family room and stood frozen in place.

"Farrah, what are they doing here?"

"They here to arrest you, Rafiq. I told them the truth," Farrah said, standing close to the detective. She looked over at Rafiq. "You're a sick man and you need help."

"You fuckin' bitch. I trusted you. I gave you everything," Rafiq barked, pulling away from the officer who was in the process of cuffing him. "I loved you when your own mother didn't."

"Fuck you, Rafiq. You never loved me. All you wanted to do is control me. Well, no more. You killed Edward . . . He loved me." Tears streamed down Farrah's face. "I hate you and I hope that they put you under the jail. I'm going to testify against you . . . I'm not scared of you . . . I don't care anymore . . . I hope you rot in jail."

If looks could kill, the one he was giving Farrah would have blown her head off. "You ungrateful bitch, I loved you, I took care of you, and you do this to me. I swear I'm going to kill your ass," Rafiq said, lunging forward. One of the officers took his baton from his waist and struck Rafiq in the back of the legs with it, causing him to fall to the ground on his knees. Farrah hid behind the detective.

"Don't worry, where he's going you won't have to worry about him for a long time," the detective said, looking over his shoulder at Farrah. "Take 'im out, boys."